Phil Re

the lives and loves of
FINN

Also available from Channel 4 Books

Hollyoaks: Luke's Secret Diary

Phil Redmond's

HOLLYOAKS

A MERSEY TELEVISION COMPANY

the lives and loves of
FINN

GERALDINE RYAN

First published 2000 by Channel 4 Books
an imprint of Macmillan Publishers Ltd
25 Eccleston Place, London SW1W 9NF
Basingstoke and Oxford

www.macmillan.co.uk

Associated companies throughout the world

ISBN 0 7522 7211 X

1 3 5 7 9 8 6 4 2

A CIP catalogue record for this book
is available from the British Library.

Photographs © The Mersey Television Company Limited
Typeset by Blackjacks
Printed in Great Britain by Mackays of Chatham plc, Chatham, Kent

This book accompanies the television series *Hollyoaks*
made by The Mersey Television Company for Channel 4.
Series Producer: Jo Hallows
Executive Producer: Phil Redmond

CHAPTER ONE

JUDE

'What would your ideal house be like, Finn? If you could choose, I mean?'

Carol was poring over the Des Res section of the *Hollyoaks Gazette*.

'I've never given it much consideration,' Finn mused. 'In the immortal words of the bard, anywhere I hang my hat is home.'

'Can't be much fun living on a double-decker bus, though,' commiserated Carol, referring to Finn's makeshift four-wheeled home, parked in a nearby yard.

'Tell you what, why don't you climb aboard one evening and discover the ups and downs for yourself?' he suggested, raising an eyebrow. Finn could never resist trying out his silver tongue on an attractive girl, even though, to be honest, Carol wasn't really his type. On a good day, he fancied himself as the kind of bloke who could charm the birds out of the trees – or at least out of their clothes. Thanks to his boyish grin and dishevelled good looks, he was often right.

Carol wasn't listening. She was staring ahead, one elbow on the counter, resting her head in her hand. Probably visualizing herself in a swanky canal-side apartment with pine floorboards and designer knick-knacks, thought Finn. That was women for you. Materialistic. Aspirational. Stick a copy of *Vogue* or *Country Mansions* in front of them and they want everything they see.

'I can see myself living in a castle,' Carol sighed. 'Somewhere in the wilds of Scotland. No. Changed my mind. Ireland, that's the place.'

Finn nearly choked on his coffee. He'd heard about Carol's spiritual tendencies, but he hadn't reckoned on second sight.

Carol's daytime reverie was interrupted as her boss, Jude Cunningham, the owner of Parker's Café, looked up from her accounts and glared at her.

'There are other customers, Carol, in case you need reminding,' she snapped. 'Unless you fancy being out of a job I suggest you see to table six before they go elsewhere.' She tossed Carol a sarcastic smile. 'See how long it takes you to save up for a castle when you're on benefits.'

Finn could have sworn he heard Carol mutter 'Die, bitch' under her breath, before sliding the newspaper under the counter and stalking off in the direction of table six. Probably justifiable under the circumstances. That Jude was a bit of a dragon. He stared into his cup, keeping well out of whatever it was that was going on between Carol and her boss. Always best to keep your head down under these circumstances, in his experience.

But the sound of Jude tapping her teeth with a pencil, combined with an occasional sigh of irritation from her direction, forced Finn to look up and give Carol's ogre of a boss a closer inspection. Blimey, she was a stunner. Seriously fit. Blonde, blue eyes, the face of an angel and, from what he could see, the body of a horny little devil. Mmm, much more his type. Perhaps he'd been a bit quick to think she was being unnecessarily hard on Carol. She was probably a bit stressed with all those figures, that's all. And talking of figures...

Jude caught him giving her the once-over and shot him a challenging look.

'Er...it's not just the toast that gets a grilling here, is it?' he quipped, embarrassed at being caught drooling over her considerable cleavage.

Jude narrowed her eyes and put her head to one side seductively.

'Did you want anything else?' she asked, her voice deadpan. 'A nice roll? Prime meat? Served on a bed of lettuce?'

Finn gulped. 'I'm vegetarian, actually,' he lied, attempting to cover up for his earlier leching.

'That's a pity,' Jude replied, licking her lips suggestively.

Phew, was it hot in here? If he wasn't very much mistaken, Jude was coming on to him big time. In fact, she seemed well up for it. And who was he to argue?

Carol bustled up behind him, carrying a laden tray, jostling for space. She followed Finn's gaze and snorted in disapproval as she clocked what was going on. Hastily, Finn moved out of Carol's way before she tipped the contents of the tray over him.

'Excuse me,' she snapped. 'You heard the boss. There are other customers in here beside yourself and most of them are spending a bit more money than you.'

'That's no way to speak to a customer, Carol,' Jude rebuked her. 'Honestly, you can't get the staff these days,' she said to Finn, her voice suddenly dripping honey.

Finn reckoned it was time to make a sharp exit before he got caught in the crossfire. Plus his motto was 'Always leave them wanting more'. Well, not *always*...

'Well ladies, I'd better be off,' he said, nodding at Jude and Carol. 'Bit of business to see to.'

'You'll be back later though?' Jude asked him, once more tapping her Colgate advert teeth with her pencil. 'When you've done this business of yours? Whatever it is.'

Finn gave the question some careful consideration.

'Oh, don't you worry, he'll be back,' Carol remarked sourly, scraping the soggy remains of baked beans on toast into the bin. 'Now he's seen where you keep the doggie biscuits.'

Finn beat a hasty retreat.

CHAPTER TWO

FINN'S DREAM

Finn's head was throbbing, his tongue felt like an old rugby sock and his throat was drier than the Gobi desert. Rubbing his eyes, he went over the events of last night. Jude. God, they'd put away some wine – if you could call it wine. More like anti-freeze with a French label. You could marinate your trainers in it and you'd end up with two prime fillets. He struggled on to his elbows, but his pounding head forced him to lie down again.

How had she managed to talk him into getting hold of some bits and pieces of furniture for Parker's? All that bollocks about 'We entrepreneurs have to look out for each other, Finn, it's dog eat dog out there.' And there was him thinking her visit was purely a 'social' one, the crafty minx. Although talk of 'You scratch my back and I'll scratch yours' hadn't been entirely metaphorical, as it turned out. Finn yawned and grinned at the memory.

What had woken him so early? Usually he slept like a log. That is, until an irate Tony from the video shop opposite banged on his window demanding to know how much longer he was expected to take his messages and when did he think he'd be buying himself a mobile phone. But Tony hadn't shown his ugly face yet.

It was a dream that had woken him this time. As he lay there, the images came flooding back. Images from time long ago, when he was a child, growing up with his grandmother in Ireland. He hadn't thought about his birthplace for years. It must have been Carol who'd planted the seed of the dream, with all her talk of castles in the country yesterday.

In his dream, he hadn't been alone. Elfine was there. Elfine: his best friend, before his father had turned up to 'snatch him away from his grandmother's clutches' – as the old bugger had described the loving upbringing the old lady had given him after the death of his own mother.

In this dream, he and Elfine were in the garage, hiding as usual from the butler, James, who would have sent Elfine packing back to the village if he'd suspected she was on Grandmother's land. Officious old sod, he was. More than a touch of the Tony about him. James had always treated that castle as if it belonged to him, not to his employer, Finn's grandmother. Well, as far as Finn was concerned he was welcome to it. Finn certainly didn't want it. Never had.

Elfine and he had been messing about in the beautifully maintained old classic car – a car only ever driven by James, and then only twice a week, once to take his grandmother to church and once to her whist drive. In those days, that car had been their hiding place.

'When I'm older I'm going to drive away in this car and never come back,' he used to tell Elfine. Strange how he hadn't thought about those days for years, yet in his dream everything had seemed so familiar.

Even then, at such a young age, he couldn't wait to get away from that draughty old castle. It was his dream to drive off somewhere, to find an old hut or a cave to live in, where people didn't treat him differently just because one day he would be Lord Kildiggin.

He didn't want to be a lord, with all those people kow-towing and being polite. He wanted to live a life like Elfine's – an ordinary life, like everyone in the village did. Everyone bar himself and his grandmother, of course.

Last night, in his dream, he'd heard Elfine's teasing laughter.

'You'll be back one day, Rory Finnigan,' she'd said. 'Back to claim this castle and your title. You'll be too grand for the likes of me then, Lord Kildiggin.'

'I'll never be Lord Kildiggin,' he swore.

'You haven't got any choice,' she insisted. 'It's your grandmother's will. She has no son, only one daughter – your mother – and she's dead. The title will be yours one day, Rory Finnigan, and there's no use fighting it.'

In his dream he got angry. Just the way he used to in reality, when the truth of her words couldn't be denied, but was also too much to cope with.

'Then I'll never come back at all!' he'd yelled in his dream. And then he'd pushed Elfine so hard she'd fallen against the steering wheel. What was it that had woken him at that point? Was it her cry of pain or the hurt look in her eyes when he told her he'd never return?

As it turned out, he hadn't realized how soon his angry words would come true. Not long after this incident, his father had come for him and taken him away back to England with him.

'You'll lead a very different life now, Rory,' were his grandmother's parting words. 'Now that you have your father to show you the difference between right and wrong.'

Finn, now fully awake, recalled how excited he'd

been at the prospect of going to England and how much he'd looked forward to leading this 'very different life'.

But that was before he'd discovered what kind of man his father really was.

CHAPTER THREE

GIVE ME THE MOONLIGHT

Jude had invited Finn to Anglesey for a long weekend. Well, not just him, to be honest, the whole gang would be there, which meant avoiding Tony and one or two others he'd rather not be cast away on a desert island with. But with things shaping up nicely between him and Jude, the trip had potential.

She was definitely after him. He could tell from the way she always refilled his coffee cup when he popped into Parker's, without him ever having to ask. And how did he feel about her? Admittedly, she was tough and abrasive, and could be cruel sometimes, but Finn was sure it was all just a front. If anyone could bring out her softer side, he felt sure he was the man for the job. With a girl as gorgeous as Jude, it had to be worth a try.

Finn had got over the dream as quickly as his hangover. He was never miserable for long. Far better to live in the present, he firmly believed. He wasn't going to let any dream haunt him. Business was picking up, and since, in Jude's eyes, he'd surpassed himself with his endeavours to refurbish Parker's, his love life looked like it wasn't far behind.

Truly, Finn decided, as he threw the remains of his breakfast into one of Tony's bins, my cup runneth over. Come to think of it, so did Jude's. And an extremely pleasant sight to behold that was too.

Not that he intended spending all his time with Jude. He'd take the opportunity to catch up with his old mate Jambo and, in the process, see if he couldn't talk him into handing over the keys to his shed – perfect for storing the furniture Finn made a living buying and selling – on a permanent basis. Yes, his luck was in, whichever way you looked at it. Finn sniffed the air appreciatively. The sun was shining and the five-day forecast was good.

There was one small blip on what was otherwise a clear horizon. Jude hadn't actually handed much over in the way of hard cash in return for the furniture he'd procured for her. But, later, as she took her seat on the bus and flashed him one of her knowing smiles, there was a glint in her eye that suggested she'd be delivering a different type of reward during their little jaunt to Anglesey.

The journey was uneventful enough, apart from having to stop twice because Carol felt sick. Everyone was in high spirits. He even managed to stop Jude worrying about how Parker's would survive with both her and Carol away.

Later on that day, Finn and Jude found themselves alone. Jambo had dragged everyone along to a beach party to listen to a band he'd heard about. The music had been loud and the booze was flowing. Somehow, they'd got detached from the rest of the party, though neither of them was complaining, especially as they'd also managed to detach a bottle of wine and a couple of glasses. The wine was making Finn lyrical, as it often did. He prided himself on being something of a self-taught philosopher. Even more so after necking large amounts of alcohol.

'D'you know, Jude,' he slurred, refilling her glass, 'I have to say this…'

Jude giggled as Finn poured wine into his own glass, a touch unsteadily.

'Here –' he waved the bottle around to show it the view, 'lying in the shelter of this sand dune with you, watching the sun slide behind the dark blue ribbon of sea, with the smell of salt on the air and the sound of waves lapping the shore – is as near to heaven as I've been in a long time.'

'You trying to butter me up, Finn?' Jude lay back in the sand and giggled again.

'You've been in the catering trade too long, my girl,' Finn replied. 'All this talk of dairy products.'

'Just when I'd almost managed to leave Parker's behind,' Jude sighed, but she was too drunk to be angry with Finn for reminding her of all the potential disasters she'd left at home. 'Do you think Kevin will be managing OK?'

Finn doubted whether Jude's intellectually challenged third-in-command was capable of organizing a piss-up in a brewery, but instinct told him that now was not the time to plant the seeds of doubt in Jude's mind.

'Piece of cake, Jude,' he insisted. 'Any idiot can run a café.'

'Cheers, Finn.'

Oops. Was it him or had some warmth gone out of Jude's voice?

'No, no.' He realized how dismissive he must have sounded. 'I didn't mean that.'

Jude waited in a brooding silence. She was an expert at that, Finn noticed. Most women were, he'd discovered.

He started back-pedalling furiously, hoping he hadn't blown his chances.

'I just meant,' he spluttered, 'that serving was the easy bit. What you do, Jude – the thinking, the planning, the organizing – now that's hard.'

'Shut up, Finn.'

Oh, dear. This wasn't going to plan. He tried the old 'personality massage' technique.

'You really have to learn to delegate, Jude. Learn to switch off now and then. You live on your nerves, you know. It's because you're a high achiever.'

'I said shut up, Finn. Why don't you come and lie down next to me? The view's brilliant from here. All those twinkly little stars.'

'Right,' Finn said. 'You're on.'

And that was only the first of many occasions that night that Finn saw stars.

CHAPTER FOUR

CAROL'S BLUES

There was an atmosphere in Parker's you could cut with a knife. Finn would have gone elsewhere for his mid-morning repast, but there was nowhere else he could get credit. Carol was buffing the tables so energetically, Finn half expected to see sawdust flying off them.

'Keep away from me with that cloth,' Finn joked as she approached his table, 'I've had a good wash this morning already.'

Not even a glimmer of a smile. She'd been decidedly off with him ever since the journey back to Hollyoaks from Anglesey. He couldn't for the life of him think what he'd done to upset her.

Jude's moods he could cope with. She shouted, she swore, she gave everyone who came within striking distance a vicious tongue-lashing. Then it was all over.

Carol was a different matter. She brooded. He could feel her eyes boring holes in the back of his neck, but when he turned round she was always looking some-where else. She looked defeated, Finn decided, like a wounded animal. And he had no idea why.

'Can I get you anything?'

Finn considered the question. 'I don't suppose a smile and a cheery word are on the menu today?'

'Sorry,' she snapped. 'I ran out of smiles when I got my wages docked and cheery words are off. Indefinitely.'

'Sit down, Carol. Just for a moment,' Finn said softly.

Carol registered no emotion on her face. 'I'm in enough trouble with the Black Witch already. If she sees me sitting down that'll be my job gone.'

'Oh, go on. Stop being a martyr.' Finn put on a camp voice. 'Sackcloth and ashes are so last season,' he lisped.

Carol smiled tentatively, then, with a quick check that Jude hadn't come in, she sat down.

'She drives a hard bargain that girl,' Finn said. 'Is she still making you work for nothing after that fiasco Kevin caused?'

They'd got back from Anglesey to discover that Parker's had been closed all weekend because dopey Kevin hadn't been able to get the key into the lock properly to let himself in. Finn surmised that, on this evidence, the poor boy's sexual prowess was likely to be limited, but had wisely kept this observation to himself. Jude had been in no mood for innuendo. She'd been far too concerned with how much profit she'd lost. And now poor Carol was having to forfeit a week's wages for Kevin's incompetence.

'There's no justice,' Carol sighed. 'And on top of this I'll probably never see Beryl again.' A tear slid down her cheek and she licked it away.

Finn felt a sudden rush of tenderness towards Carol. She looked so depressed and vulnerable, he almost felt like giving her a reassuring hug.

'It was bad luck Beryl going over the cliff like that,' he commiserated. 'Just when you'd passed your test, too.'

Beryl was Carol's car – a ridiculous three-wheeler she inexplicably loved to bits. Carol had left her perilously close to the edge of a cliff and had forgotten to put the handbrake on. Where once Beryl, the yellow peril, had hurtled down the motorway at speeds of – oh – thirty miles per hour, she was now a soggy, waterlogged mess.

'My pride and joy,' Carol sniffed. 'All that money I spent on lessons. All that time I spent sprucing her up. And now what have I got to show for it?'

'Well, if there's anything I can do, Carol,' he offered. 'If you need a lift anywhere, or anything.'

'That's sweet of you, Finn,' Carol said. 'I wish everyone was as understanding.'

Finn had an inkling who she meant by 'everyone'.

All of a sudden, Carol jumped up and pulled her notepad and pencil from her apron pocket.

'Oh, God.' She was a bag of nerves once more. 'Jude's heading this way. Quick, order something.'

Jude was crossing the road on her way back to the café, her face its usual mask of inscrutability. Then Finn's stomach gave a lurch. There was someone else coming out of the shop just behind her. Someone he hadn't seen in years. Someone he hoped he wouldn't be seeing in a long time. It was Eric, his dad. Finn had suddenly lost his appetite.

CHAPTER FIVE

ERIC'S RETURN

Eric Finnigan had a criminal record as long as the M6. Committing petty crime was, he claimed, just a bad habit he could stop if he wanted to. Trouble is, he never wanted to.

'Seen much of your grandmother recently, son? Unless the old bitch has popped her clogs and I haven't been informed of the happy event.'

'Dad, don't.'

Finn had always been close to his gran in spirit, even though he'd never been much of a letter-writer and she disliked the phone. He couldn't stand the way his father talked about her, though to be honest, it wasn't surprising. The way she talked about him was even worse. For an old lady, her choice of expletives was highly imaginative.

Eric Finnigan, according to his grandmother, was born a rogue and would die a rogue. He'd married her only daughter for her money and her connections, then brought her down to his own level. It was a blessing in disguise that she'd died when she did, according to Gran, because at least it meant she was spared any further misery.

According to Eric, however, things had been very

different – as he proceeded to remind Finn for the hundredth time.

'Your mother hated that castle,' he said. 'She was a free spirit, Finn. Just like me. She knew what she was doing when she ran away and married me. She was leaving that old bitch behind and everything she represented.'

'Yes, Dad,' Finn sighed. He knew from experience there was no point in challenging his dad when he got on to this topic

'They made her go back, after all that nonsense with that jewellery they found on me,' Eric continued. 'Planted it on me, she did, the evil old witch, and that's God's honest truth.'

Finn doubted his father would recognize God's honest truth if it came and smacked him in the face with a wet kipper. He'd lost any illusions about his old man a long time ago. Now he saw him for what he was: trouble.

'I've had the police round asking if I've seen you,' Finn hissed, doing his best to remain calm.

They were sitting in the darkest recess of Parker's, but Finn was jumpy nonetheless.

'Is that a fact?' Eric sounded almost proud.

'You have escaped from the nick, Dad,' Finn reminded him. 'They didn't just let you out so you could pay a little visit to your turf accountant, stock up on fags and booze, then take in some quality time with your son.'

'Speaking of which, you haven't got a fag on you, have you, son? Only I seem to remember I had my last tab ripped from behind my ear by Big Jim Blood just before I – er – left my previous address. Lucky encounter, that.'

'How come?' Finn couldn't help being intrigued.

'Person before me didn't smoke,' he said. 'Big Jim had his ear instead.'

As always when he wanted something, his father turned on the charming smile. Not that it ever worked with Finn.

It was working with Jude, though. Even now, Eric was following her every move with his beady eyes. Surely the old sod didn't think he had a chance with her, thought Finn. Anyway, he'd soon find out that Jude only ever smiled at people if she thought she could get something for nothing out of them.

'Have a glass of wine with me, Eric. You too, Finn, of course.'

Finn's mouth dropped open at the sight of Jude bearing down on the two of them, a bottle in one hand and three wineglasses in the other. Jesus, it was true, then. Jude was after something. And if he knew his father – which he did only too well – then whatever it was, it was bound to be dodgy.

'Don't mind if I do,' Eric said, rubbing his hands together in gleeful anticipation of a free drink.

'I'll pass, if you don't mind,' said Finn. 'I've got a busy day tomorrow.'

His father didn't even have the grace to pretend to be disappointed that Finn wouldn't be staying. But Finn felt slightly less annoyed when he noticed Jude's face fall as he stood up.

'Do you have to go, Finn?' she asked him. 'Only I've got something I'd like to discuss with you.'

'Let the boy get off to his bed,' Eric said, a bit too readily. 'It's never a good idea to discuss business when you're tired.'

Now Finn was certain there was some dodgy dealing going on between his dad and Jude. But he decided to let it go for the time being. If he didn't know about it, then maybe – just maybe – it would go away.

CHAPTER SIX

DODGY DEALING

As things turned out, it didn't. Which was why Finn found himself at the wheel of his van on a warm evening in August – Jude dozing in the seat beside him – on their way back home, after a long day which had entailed first dropping Eric off at the prison gates, then a ferry crossing to France.

Finn blinked as the motorway lights began to merge into each other. Another hour and they'd be home. He was dog-tired. Typical of Jude to close her eyes and fall asleep like that, leaving him with all the driving. She stirred, stretched, yawned, then sat up.

'Here already?' she asked. 'I've just been having a lovely dream.'

'Lucky old you,' Finn muttered.

Jude smiled at him affectionately and placed her hand on his knee. He hoped she wasn't entertaining any funny ideas, because as soon he'd unloaded this lot he was off home for a kip. It wasn't like him to be reticent in these matters, but it had been a very long day and he could hardly keep his eyes open, let alone muster the energy for any strenuous action in the bedroom department.

'I expect your dad's nicely tucked up beneath his prison blanket by now,' Jude said with a sly smile.

Finn wished she'd stop making references to the fact that his dad was an escaped convict. Or rather, he had been until this morning, when they'd dropped him off with strict instructions to turn himself in…before they did.

'You'd have been laughing on the other side of your face, my girl,' he reminded her, 'if you'd allowed him to go with you across the Channel.'

Jude made a face. 'How was I to know he was serving time for smuggling booze?' she demanded. 'But thanks for stepping in, Finn. I couldn't have done this trip single-handed. I owe you one.'

Finn gave her a cheeky leer. 'You owe me more than one, mate,' he said. 'Only if you don't mind I'd rather you didn't start paying me back until tomorrow. I'm knackered.'

'Poor Finn,' Jude said with a semi-mocking smile. 'You're not really cut out for living life on the edge, are you? Hard to believe Eric's your dad.'

'Eric's just stupid,' Finn said, annoyed that anyone could compare him unfavourably to his father. 'He always gets caught. And so will you if you make a habit of this game.'

'It's illegal, I know,' she said. 'But think of the buzz, Finn.'

* * *

A sour-faced Carol helped unload the crates back at Parker's. She hated being left in the dark about things and had been trying to work out just what exactly was going on from the moment they'd all three disappeared so mysteriously that morning.

She expected the usual cavalier treatment from Jude, who never trusted her with anything but the most menial of tasks, but she had thought Finn was her friend. After all, only last week he'd driven her to Anglesey and back in order to reclaim poor Beryl, towing her all the way home. He'd even said she could keep Beryl in the yard. So why hadn't he confided in her?

All she'd learned from him was that Eric had gone back to stay with his sister, which sounded very fishy. When Jude finally came out with the news that they'd spent the day in France stocking up with wine for Parker's, Carol had practically exploded.

'How can she do this to me?' she yelled at Finn, who was having a five-minute break from lugging boxes. 'How could you both do this to me?'

'No one will find out, Carol,' Finn reassured her. 'She's promised to change the labels. And as far as I'm concerned it's the first and last time I'm ever doing that run. I swear.'

Carol was still glaring at him. 'You don't get it, do you?'

Finn clearly didn't. 'Enlighten me, Carol. Are you worried about the police?'

'Actually, no I'm not,' Carol said with mock patience. 'I couldn't give a flying one about the police. I'll let Jude worry about them. What concerns me, Finn, is that both of you went off on that little jolly without giving me one thought.'

Finn scratched his head. 'Well, if it's a bonus for the extra responsibility you've had while Jude's been away, then I'm sure you can both come to some sort of––'

Carol didn't give him a chance to finish. Instead she screamed her words: 'The least you could have done was ask me along, Finn! I don't suppose it even occurred to you that I might like to be asked, did it?'

Then, to Finn's amazement, she burst into tears.

CHAPTER SEVEN

'ALLO, 'ALLO!

'If you take any more of those travel pills you'll start rattling,' Finn joked as Carol ripped the foil off another little gold wrapper.

'I don't know why she has to sit in the middle,' Jude remarked stroppily. 'Why don't you sit near the window if you're going to throw up?'

Carol just beamed at her. Not even Jude could ruin her first visit abroad.

'I won't be sick,' she said. 'That's what the tablets are for, ignoramus!'

Jude stared out of the window, still angry with Finn for allowing Carol to take up space that could better be filled with bottles of duty-free wine.

'God knows what state Parker's will be in when we get back,' she moaned. 'Kevin's probably turning it into a soup kitchen for the homeless as I speak.'

'So that's what the tureens were for,' Finn said.

Jude threw him a look that could have stripped paint at ten paces.

'It was a joke, Jude,' Finn said patiently. 'Lighten up. Look, everybody, here's the ferry. Close your eyes while I get parked up. I usually do. It's less scary that way.'

'Finn!' Jude shrieked, gripping his arm.

Finn wondered what had happened to Jude's sense of humour recently. It had always been a bit on the short side when it came to Carol, but all she'd done since they'd got in the van this morning was to have a go at him at every opportunity.

Carol, on the other hand, was enjoying herself – and it showed. When she wasn't popping travel pills, she read out bits from her guidebook to entertain them. Jude, however, was having none of it, either cutting her off mid-sentence or coming out with withering remarks that showed herself off as a seasoned traveller and showed Carol up as a country bumpkin who'd never been further south than Birmingham.

On the ferry, Jude sulked into her cup of coffee while Carol made serious inroads into a huge baguette.

'This is like no baguette I've ever had,' she said in wonderment.

'That's because it's made with different flour from the stuff we use,' Finn informed her. 'Makes it more crusty. More crumbs.'

'How do you know that?' Carol asked him, impressed.

Finn tapped the side of his nose. 'There are more things in heaven and earth than are dreamt of in your philosophy, Carol,' was all he'd say.

'How do you say, "You're doing my head in" in French?' Jude asked, attempting to shield herself from the barrage of crumbs from Carol's baguette.

Finn smiled sweetly. 'Tu prends ma tête,' he said.

Jude scowled. 'Why we have to stay overnight I've no idea,' she said. 'This is supposed to be a business trip. All we need to do is get off the ferry, drive to a hypermarket, stock up and come home. But no, we have to stay overnight, so Carol can experience the joys of foreign travel for the first time in her pathetic little life.'

Finn frowned at her. Carol was merrily chomping away, seemingly oblivious to Jude's continual snide remarks, but Finn knew some of it must be hitting home. He'd been sticking up for her all the way but he wasn't sure how much help that was – as the more he defended her, the bitchier Jude got.

It was down to him that Carol was here in the first place. She'd been so desperate to come along that Finn didn't have the heart to refuse her a place. He'd even paid for her ticket, much to the annoyance of Jude, who'd promptly threatened to dock her wages for the day in retaliation, until Finn told her that unless she withdrew the threat, no one would be going. It was his van, after all.

Thankfully, Jude began to lighten up on the other side of the Channel. Finn insisted on taking up Carol's suggestion that they repair to a typical French café for a nice glass of wine. Jude was reluctant at first, reminding everyone that they were here to make money, not to spend it, but she was soon shouted down.

Later, Finn wondered if it was the wine that caused Jude to call off her dogs – after her second glass she managed to behave with some civility towards Carol. In fact, for a while, everything was perfect. Jude almost became infected with Carol's enthusiasm, even helping Finn to haggle for a table from the flea market on their way back to the port.

Carol was happy with everything, to Finn's relief. From the word go he had felt somehow responsible for making her first trip abroad as memorable as possible. Quite how memorable it was going to be, however, he didn't suspect, until they reached the port and were stopped at Customs.

'You'd better let me do the talking,' Finn said out of

the corner of his mouth. The Customs officer prowled suspiciously around the outside of the van, like Hercule Poirot on a case.

'I told you that flamin' table would draw attention to us,' Jude hissed. 'Look! He's going to search us now.'

And sure enough, he did.

'You know it's illegal to import wine into Britain with the express purpose of selling it on to make a profit, sir?'

Finn had to think fast. Carol was staring at her knees, guilt written over her face in letters a foot tall. Jude stared out of the window as if she were sizing up the distance between here and the nearest autoroute. There's loyalty for you, Finn thought bitterly.

Then, in a blinding flash, inspiration struck him. It often happened like that, he'd discovered over the years. He could be floundering around, up to his neck in a tricky situation – and then suddenly the perfect means of blagging his way out would present itself. He took Jude's hand and kissed it lovingly.

'Meet my fiancée, Jude.'

Jude's mouth dropped open, Carol look stunned.

'Ma chère.' Finn batted his eyes at Jude as a warning for her to keep her mouth shut, but for once both Carol and Jude were simultaneously lost for words. A definite first.

Much to Finn's relief and amazement, the officer believed his story that the wine was intended for his wedding – to Jude.

'Bonne chance!' the officer called out as he waved them on their way. 'You're a very lucky man.'

'You don't know how lucky,' Jude muttered, flashing the officer one of her stunning smiles.

'I think I need the loo,' Carol said. 'All this excitement has played havoc with my bowels. See you in the bar.'

Finn and Jude set off in search of a much-needed drink. The sea was calm and blue, and for some time they sat in the bar and said nothing, just stared out of the window, contemplating what might have been but for Finn's flash of inspiration and convincing method acting.

'Do you think we should go and have a look for Carol?' Finn said after a while. 'She's been gone ages.'

There was no need. A flustered looking Carol was already on her way over, having just made an extremely worrying discovery. It seemed that contraband booze wasn't the only thing hidden in Finn's van.

CHAPTER EIGHT

THE END OF THE AFFAIR

After a silence so deep and uncomfortable you could hardly breathe – which lasted until they'd dropped off their three stowaways and let themselves into a deserted Parker's – the floodgates opened and Jude finally started to lay into Finn and Carol. To Finn it came almost as a relief. The waiting had been a nightmare.

'Gone. Two dozen bottles nicked,' Jude said.

'She seemed like a nice woman, Jude,' Carol said. 'I thought I was doing you a favour. It was your brother and his stupid mates who were stowing away in the back of the van, after all. I told you I thought I could hear noises on the way over, didn't I?'

Jude glared at her.

'And you accused Carol of being jumpy because she'd taken too many travel tablets, didn't you, Jude?' Finn intervened. 'You should have listened to her.'

'Shut up, you.'

Finn figured it was wise to do as she said.

'I was only trying to protect them from the police,' Carol persisted. It turned out that when Jude and Finn had gone to the bar at Calais, Carol had caught Jude's

- 33 -

little brother and his two mates trying to sneak back into the van. She'd taken pity on them and agreed not to grass them up to Jude. The problem was, with the van now crammed with wine, there was no room for the three stowaways. Fortunately – or so it had seemed – a kindly woman Carol had met earlier in the day stepped in to help them out of the jam.

'So let me get this straight, Carol,' said Jude, her voice dripping with sarcasm. 'You trusted a complete stranger to fill her car with our wine with some stupid promise of meeting up with her later at a filling station to get it back off her.'

After days of biting his tongue, Finn finally lost his rag. 'Yeah, so that your blockhead of a brother and his divvy mates – who didn't have a penny between them to get back home on the bus – could come back with us in the van,' he reminded her. 'Don't you have any family feelings, Jude? They would have been arrested if they'd been caught on the ferry with no tickets.'

'It would have served them right!'

Jude itched to have another go at her kid brother.

'Anyway,' Carole ventured, cowering behind Finn's six-foot-three frame. 'She wasn't a complete stranger. She was called Alice and she came from Nuneaton.'

'And she's probably back in bloody Nuneaton at this very moment knocking back a glass of my flamin' wine!' Jude screamed. 'Meanwhile I'm down by two hundred quid.'

She gave an ironic laugh. 'And to think I was under the impression that the purpose of a booze cruise was to make a profit.'

When Finn reminded Jude that there was also her share of the petrol money to cough up, Jude went ballistic. Carol thought this was a good moment to leave.

She just hoped Finn would be able to cope on his own.

Finn decided that if he was going to be at the receiving end of Jude's whiplash tongue, he might as well go the whole hog. Might as well be hung for a sheep as for a lamb, eh? And basically, he was past caring by now.

'There's also one or two other outstanding accounts,' he reminded her, referring to the furniture he'd got hold of for Parker's, which Jude still hadn't coughed up for.

Jude did a double take. 'Outstanding accounts? Are you mad?'

'Not mad, Jude. Just skint and thoroughly pissed off with the way you seem to think you're the only person who needs money to live.'

Jude opened her mouth wide and then shut it again, before finally striding over to the till and dramatically ringing it open.

'How much do I owe you?' she snapped.

Timidly, Finn presented her with a neatly written invoice. Jude snatched it from him and slapped the money she owed on to the counter.

'That's that, then,' she said.

Finn gathered that she wasn't just referring to their business transaction. He was hit by a sudden wave of relief. Until now, he hadn't fully realized how exhausting having a relationship with Jude was, gorgeous though she might be.

As he made his way to the door, Finn couldn't resist a parting shot. 'Carol's right about you,' he said. 'You're only interested in money and what you can get out of people.'

'Not bloody Carol again,' Jude said, brushing off his accusation. She'd heard that one too many times from other people to let it worry her much any more. 'Carol, Carol, Carol. Do you fancy her or something?'

Finn thought about it. Did he?

'Of course I don't,' he said. 'Carol's a friend, that's all. A friend. Look it up in the dictionary, Jude. It's a word you've still not managed to define.'

'Shut the door on your way out, Finn,' Jude said.

Finn smiled at her sweetly. 'It'll be my pleasure,' he replied.

And it was with some satisfaction that Finn let himself out on to the street and made his way home.

CHAPTER NINE

QUESTIONS

That night, in bed, Finn went over the conversation he'd just had with Jude. Did he fancy Carol? Did she fancy him? Surely not. He thought back to the times they'd been alone together. What if she'd been reading things into those occasions that weren't actually there?

First of all there'd been Anglesey. And Beryl. When Carol had asked Finn to teach her to check the oil in her car, had it been her way of getting him on his own? He'd been up to his elbows in oil, he remembered – in no fit state to make a move on a girl.

It was while she was messing about looking for tissues so that he could clean some of the oil off, that the car had somehow rolled backwards over the edge of the cliff into the sea. Okay, so he'd given her a reassuring hug afterwards, and Jude hadn't been very pleased when she'd turned up at that inopportune moment – mistaking friendship for sex, as usual. But surely he'd only done what anyone would have done. Carol had been grief-stricken. Beryl was the only thing she owned. She'd sunk her life savings into that car.

Then, only last week, he'd gone back with her to retrieve Beryl from the garage. They'd had a lovely day. Without Jude's constant sniping, Finn was able to relax in Carol's company. She'd really opened up that day, telling him funny stories about growing up in Bury, then progressing to sad tales about how useless Jude made her feel.

Had he said anything to give her the wrong idea about his feelings towards her? He racked his brains. He'd told her she was sweet, that was one thing. But he'd only been telling the truth. She was sweet. He'd also told her that she was an excellent waitress.

'It's not easy to do what you do,' he recalled saying. 'Number crunching and ordering enough food to go round – now that's the easy bit. But you're at the coal-face, Carol. You're the one who has to deal with the difficult customers. It's you they complain to first, not Jude.'

He'd said it to cheer her up – to get her off her obsession with Jude. What was there to misinterpret about that?

Then he remembered the other things he'd said.

'I can't help comparing myself to Jude and coming second, Finn,' Carol had said as they munched their sandwiches in a lay-by on the way home. 'I mean, look at her. She's got everything. Legs that go up to her armpits, gorgeous white teeth.'

'Nice pair of fetlocks,' Finn added. 'She's not a horse, Carol.'

Carol nodded in agreement. 'No,' she said. 'That's entirely the wrong animal. The one I'm thinking of barks and stays out all night.'

'I'm not going to slag Jude off just to make you feel better, Carol,' Finn said. 'I never talk about people behind their backs – unless it's Tony of course, and he's fair game.' Carol nodded in agreement. It was a fair point. 'But I'll listen without passing comment if it helps to get it off your chest.'

'And that's another thing,' Carol went on. 'That cleavage. You can't imagine how often I have to go over that counter with a J-cloth after a day of male customers drooling all over it.'

'Oh, come on, Carol.' Finn tried to console her. 'Big tits aren't everything.' OK, so that statement wasn't entirely true, he thought to himself, but what harm was there in a little white lie if it made Carol feel better?

'Jude's got the kind of figure that's at its peak right now, that's all,' he continued. 'In another ten or fifteen years – after she's had a couple of kids – she'll probably run completely to fat. Whereas you, Carol,' he offered her a bag of prawn cocktail-flavoured crisps, 'will remain as petite and perky as you are now. Precious things come in small packages – that's what my old gran always says.'

Was it this remark that had caused Carol to think he fancied her? Carol hadn't mentioned Jude for the rest of the journey, apart from referring to her as 'old saggy tits' once or twice.

Back in the present, Finn punched his pillow to get comfortable. It was almost daylight already and he hadn't had a wink of sleep yet. No, he'd got it wrong about Carol. As far as she was concerned, he was the big brother she'd never had, that was all. First thing tomorrow he'd volunteer to do a bit of repair work on Beryl – see if he couldn't get her ship-shape before Christmas. He'd have plenty of time on his hands now that Jude and he were finished.

CHAPTER TEN

A LETTER FROM IRELAND

Dear Rory,

It's been a long time since I've been in touch with you. This is not to say that you haven't been very much in my thoughts recently. I hope you are keeping well and remembering to wrap up warm – I remember those chesty coughs you used to have as a boy! Well, how could I not – I was kept awake at nights most winters with your continual hacking! I hope and trust you've grown out of your poor health now, Rory. Some things, however, can only get worse and not better with age.

My poor heart, unfortunately, grows weaker all the time. Sometimes at night I lie awake and wonder how much longer I have left on this earth. I don't think it will be too long, Rory, before I am reunited with your dear mother in heaven. Meanwhile, I live out my meagre life in the hope of witnessing you take up your rightful place as my heir.

There have always been Kildiggins at Kildiggin Castle ever since Queen Elizabeth the First herself entrusted the care of this estate to the first Lord Kildiggin. I would not rest in my grave if I thought the estate were to go to rack and ruin, all because you were too proud to re-think those careless words you used to speak when you were a child.

How like your mother you always were, Rory! Property is theft, mother, she used to say. Well, as I told her – there is no thief like the Government's tax men, Rory, and it will be those thieves who inherit this estate, unless you are prepared to put your misguided principles aside.

Don't break my heart like she did. Come home. There are so many things we need to resolve before I die.

You are welcome here any time, you know that. Bring your friends – I'm sure you have many, you always were a sociable boy. But make it soon, my darling grandson. Once I am in my grave it will be too late for us.

Your loving Grandmother.

Finn folded the letter back into its envelope and shoved it into his jacket pocket. He suddenly felt like he was carrying a huge weight on his shoulders, the crushing burden of responsibility – something he'd spent many years skilfully avoiding.

It was clear even from a cursory reading of his grandmother's words that she had the bit very firmly between her teeth. There was only one way to confront her when she was in this kind of mood and that was with the support of a posse of mates. On his own he was no match for the old lady, weak heart or no weak heart.

But how was he going to explain to everyone that far from being the ordinary – though not *that* ordinary, he liked to think – Finn they all knew and loved, he was in fact the future Lord Kildiggin? It would change everything.

He tried to imagine Lewis's face when he told him. Lewis was his business partner, after all. He might start to wonder, if Finn had kept this up his sleeve for so long, what other little details he might be keeping from him.

And what about the girls? How was he to know if it was him they couldn't keep their hands off, and not the family heirlooms? Some girls would do anything if they thought they were in with a chance of becoming Lady Kildiggin.

Hang on a minute – was that such a bad thing? Suddenly realizing the massive pulling potential he'd been passing up all this time, Finn slapped his forehead with the flat of his hand. What a fool he'd been!

'Have a word with yourself, Finn,' he muttered.

Suddenly images of beautiful young women lining up for the honour of being Lord Kildiggin's girlfriend started to take shape in his mind. Right, then. He'd ask all the girls he knew. A busload. OK, so he wasn't sure if he actually knew a busload. But there was Carol. And the rest of the gang of course. They could all go with him to Ireland and see the truth for themselves.

CHAPTER ELEVEN

SEA FEVER

Finn and Carol were taking the air, swaying from side to side as they bowled along the first-class deck. It had been Finn's idea to pass themselves off as first-class passengers. The boat was at its steadiest there, he'd said, which was vital for Carol, who felt nauseous stepping into a puddle.

'Just peer down your nose if some jobsworth looks as if he might be coming over to check your ticket,' Finn advised.

Walking and eating were the only activities Carol could contemplate when she was ocean bound. How people could choose a cruise for their honeymoon was a mystery to her. Lewis and Ruth had disappeared into a cabin the moment they'd boarded the ship. The very thought made Carol queasy.

'You've been really quiet all the way down, Finn,' Carol said. 'Is there anything up?'

'Keep your eyes on the horizon, Carol,' Finn advised her, skilfully sidestepping her question. 'It's the one thing you can be certain will remain constant.'

Carol wasn't so sure. It seemed to dip quite dramatically at moments, before picking itself up and keeling off in the opposite direction. Just like her stomach, in fact.

'Do you mind if we stop walking?' she asked Finn. 'Only I need to close my eyes for a bit.'

Finn was quite relieved too. He couldn't work out how to say what he wanted to say and walk while remaining upright at the same time. He'd wanted to put Carol in the picture about where exactly they were going before he told the others, since before they'd boarded the ferry. But where to start?

'The last time you and me were on a ferry was soon after you and Jude split up,' Carol reminded him.

'Well, we've all passed a lot of water since then,' Finn said.

'Do you miss her?' Carol could be dreadfully persistent.

'Miss who?'

Carol almost smiled – though distinctly green around the gills. 'It was really nice of you to ask us to come to Ireland with you, Finn,' she said. 'You're a really generous guy, do you know that?'

Finn shrugged a 'who, me?' shrug and scratched his tousled mop of hair. He hoped everyone would feel the same when they found out his little secret.

'It's the least I could do,' he said. 'You have to work at keeping your mates, after all.'

He hoped Carol would get the hint that he was referring to her.

'Well, you'll have to work a lot harder at keeping Tony after the way you've treated him,' Carol said.

Finn realized she hadn't got it at all. He smiled wanly.

'Tony's an exception,' he said.

Carol nodded. 'So that excuses you pinching his electricity all those months and worrying him sick about who's going to take over Store 24 plus all the other crap you've given him?'

Finn and Lewis had wound Tony up by telling him that Store 24 – which had closed down when the owner had died – was going to reopen as an undertaker's. They'd taken it further by sticking a coffin outside his front door, with a message asking him to take care of it until the undertaker opened for business and was in a position to reclaim it.

'The coffin was empty, Carol,' Finn said, faking a wounded expression.

The two remained silent for a few moments, looking out to sea. Finn decided to take the bull by the horns and finally speak his mind.

'I've been thinking, Carol,' he said, at last. 'This holiday might be just the right opportunity for us to get to know each other a little better in the more relaxed environment of – er – my family home.'

Carol's eyes were shut again, he noticed. She was going a funny colour. He wasn't sure if she suited green. He decided to take advantage of her silence. It was not often that he was presented with such a prolonged opportunity to get a word in edgewise when he was with Carol.

'We've had a few crossed wires over the last few months,' he went on, encouraged by Carol's silence. He peered out to sea once more, so that he wouldn't be distracted by her face. 'But you must know that I really like you and I'm not wrong, am I, in feeling that you like me too?'

'Can we find somewhere to lie down, Finn?' Carol asked, in a small voice.

Finn had never had Carol down as the fast type – she'd always been a bit shy in that department, he thought – but if that was what the girl wanted...

'I'm sure there must be somewhere...'

'It's too late,' Carol groaned, as she threw up in glorious Technicolor over the railing.

CHAPTER TWELVE

KILDIGGIN CASTLE

'This is never it,' Carol said, as the first glimpse of Kildiggin Castle came into view.

'I thought we were camping,' Tony said. 'I even brought my Primus stove.'

'You're having a laugh, aren't you, Finn?' a gob-smacked Lewis asked him. 'Now just let me turn this bus round and we'll soon be heading for the nearest camp-site. Come on everybody, back in your seats. It's just Finn pulling one of his little stunts.'

But, when they caught sight of James the butler tottering towards them in his penguin suit and white gloves, it became abundantly clear that, far from pulling a stunt, for once Finn was telling the truth.

'Who's the ancient drone?' Carol wondered aloud.

'Welcome home, Lord Kildiggin,' the old man quavered, reaching out with shaky hands for Finn's bag. 'Lady Molly is waiting for you in the library.'

'Lady Molly?' Carol pinched herself. 'Library?'

'Perhaps you'll help with the ladies' luggage,' Finn said. 'These gentlemen are more than capable of carrying their own stuff.'

'Oh, I don't know,' Tony said.

Finn silenced him with a stern look. His holiday

mood was sinking fast at the prospect of a meeting with his grandmother. He knew that after the usual preamble of 'lovely to see you' and 'my, haven't you grown', she would soon be back on the usual subject – his inheritance.

On top of that, he had to deal with the already changing attitude of his friends. Lewis had a gleam in his eye which Finn recognized as his 'how can I get the best wind-up out of this situation' look. Tony was smiling at him and being nice, which made Finn feel extremely queasy. Tony being nasty he could cope with – but Tony being nice? It made his flesh crawl just to think of it.

And Carol? Well, she was looking distinctly odd. And just when he thought he'd managed to get her to trust him again.

'I was just about to tell you everything only you threw up,' he told her, shame-faced.

'If it's all the same to you I think I need a lie down,' she said. 'But I'm not sleeping in that castle. It's creepy.'

Tony and Lewis grabbed an arm each and propelled her inside, the others shuffling in behind her, too awe-struck to speak.

'You'll be fine, Carol,' Tony said. 'You've got Kate and Lucy here to look after you. And if any of you girls feel the slightest bit scared during the night, you only have to call my name.'

Privately, Carol thought she'd rather be ravaged by a headless horseman, but she kept her thoughts to herself.

Once Finn had shown everyone to their respective rooms, he trotted along obediently to see his grandmother.

'I won't be staying in the castle, Gran, if it's all the same to you,' he said once the formalities were out of the way. 'I'll be sleeping on the bus for as long as I'm here.'

His grandmother's face fell. 'Not that silly talk again, Rory,' she said. 'I'd hoped to persuade you to stay on this time. For ever. I'm not getting any younger, you know.'

'You'll go on longer than me, Gran,' Finn joked.

But even as he spoke, he couldn't help noticing how much his gran had aged since he had last seen her. Her vigorous voice had faded almost to a whisper and her once upright frame had shrunk to skeletal proportions. He noticed too how dilapidated some of the rooms were looking. Presumably the estate was eating away at his grandmother's finances. Either she couldn't afford the upkeep any longer, or poor old James, who was looking even more decrepit than the last time he'd seen him, simply didn't have the energy and strength to carry out his gran's housekeeping orders any more.

* * *

After a mercifully uneventful night's sleep, the debate over Finn's duties at future Lord Kildiggin raged on the next morning.

'I may not be the person to persuade you to stay on, Rory,' his grandmother continued, 'but there's someone coming to dinner tonight who may.'

Finn was intrigued.

'You remember Elfine, don't you?'

Finn nodded.

'Well, she'll be here later, so I hope you'll be polite to her, Rory. She's a beautiful young girl these days.'

Finn doubted it. He'd loved Elfine dearly as a friend all those years ago, but of all the words there were in the world to describe her – outgoing, fun, bubbly, smart – the word 'beautiful' wasn't one of them.

But the fact is that chubby, bespectacled little girls with fat, dirty knees and gaps where their front teeth should be can sometimes metamorphose into blonde babes with a wicked gleam in their eye, as Finn was to discover that evening over dinner.

CHAPTER THIRTEEN

A DEATH

Whatever new leaf Finn had decided to turn over regarding Carol seemed to shrivel up as soon as Elfine walked into the room that evening. She bewitched everyone present, apart from Carol, whose eyes were daggers over the dining table. Finn casually enquired if Elfine had a boyfriend.

'Do you remember Connor O'Brien?' she said.

Finn vaguely remembered a fat boy with owlish glasses who always came top of the class and sneered at Finn's English accent. 'Wasn't he the doctor's son?' he asked.

Elfine nodded. 'He was,' she said. 'And now he's the doctor. Your gran's doctor, actually.'

'It must be a relief, Finn,' Carol said sarcastically, 'to think that Elfine's not been pining away all these years just waiting for you to make a reappearance in her life.'

It was late when everyone went to bed. Carol was convinced that the castle had bad vibes and begged Finn to let her sleep on the bus, but Finn was in no mood for her insecurities – regarding ghosts or anything else.

He suspected that given half a chance she'd pretty soon steer the conversation round to Elfine and she wouldn't be happy until she'd forced Finn to admit that he found her attractive. Always the happy-go-lucky type, he was starting to feel that he wasn't as on top of things as he usually was – something to do with being in his old home and in his grandmother's company again after all this time. He knew he wouldn't stand a chance against Carol once she started on him.

On top of that, he couldn't escape the fact that his grandmother was measuring him up as a suitable heir. They'd gone over her dying wishes at length already and Finn suspected that tomorrow would bring more of the same. All he needed was to drink as much wine as he could and then pass out until late the next morning.

Unfortunately, Finn's wish was not to be granted. It was the middle of the night, or so it seemed, when he was dragged from sleep by a loud and insistent knocking on the door of the bus.

'Finn! Wake up!' Finn recognized Tony's distraught yelling. 'It's your grandmother! I think she's had a heart attack. You've got to come up to the castle. Someone's already called the doctor. He's on his way.'

The new doctor, Elfine's boyfriend, taller, slimmer and without the owlish glasses now, was waiting for Finn in his grandmother's bedroom with the news that it was too late – his grandmother had passed away.

'I didn't realize how ill she was,' Finn said, disoriented from having been woken up so suddenly and still reeling with the shock.

'No, you wouldn't have,' Connor said, a smile of self-satisfaction playing on his lips. 'It's not as if you were a regular visitor hereabouts.'

It crossed Finn's mind that young Connor O'Brien – whom he'd hated on sight – might well have had designs on his grandmother's will. Was that why he'd danced attendance at her every whim since his father had retired, as Elfine had hinted over dinner? Well, he'd be sorely disappointed when he read it, Finn thought. There was only one person mentioned in that will and that was himself. The old lady had won, like she always did. He was Lord Kildiggin whether he liked it or not. Finn felt a brief rush of sympathy for his father who had also always come off second best in any battle of wills with his grandmother.

'My grandmother had a wish to sail on the lake one last time before being put to rest in her coffin,' he said soberly. 'I intend carrying out her request tomorrow. Thank you for everything you've done, Doctor. I'm sure you'll want to be getting home to your bed now.'

Finn saw the doctor out politely but firmly and then made his way into the dining room to pour himself a stiff whiskey. He wouldn't get back to sleep now, and besides he had some thinking to do. For one thing, he wouldn't be going back to England with the others. He was Lord Kildiggin, after all. And he had a funeral to organize.

CHAPTER FOURTEEN

ELFINE

'So, Rory. They've gone.'

'When are you going to start calling me Finn, Elfine? Nobody calls me Rory any more, remember?'

'Your grandmother did,' Elfine reminded him.

Finn and Elfine were alone now that the last of the few funeral guests had departed.

'I'll do my best to remember – Finn.'

She watched Finn scraping the remains of the funeral food into the bin.

'Leave the mess,' she said. 'James will clear up. Why don't we go for a walk before it gets dark? It's a lovely afternoon and it's so dark and dismal in here with the blinds down and everything.'

Finn nodded in gloomy agreement, glad to be spared the chores. He'd felt uncomfortable, trussed up in a black tie and suit jacket all day. He didn't own either, so he'd been forced to borrow them from the smarmy Connor, who'd been only too happy to show off the contents of his wardrobe. He removed the two offending items with a sigh of relief and grabbed his own much-cherished shabby jacket.

Outside the air was sharp and clean. Finn stomped along the gravel, his brain whirring with conflicting emotions and tough decisions to be made. Funerals were such depressing events, for all their talk about heaven and angels. For the first time since she'd died, he realized that he'd never see his grandmother again. It was such an obvious thought, but one that hadn't actually occurred to him until this moment.

Elfine grabbed his arm and shook it hard. 'Come on, Finn,' she said. 'Snap out of it. Smell the pine. Aren't you just glad to be alive on a day like this?' Immediately she realized what she'd said and put her hand to her mouth. 'Oh, Finn, I'm so sorry,' she said.

Perhaps it was the look of abject contrition on her face that did it. Or maybe it was because she looked so stunning, dressed as she was from head to toe in black, the swathe of her velvet hooded cloak enfolding her petite figure and elfin face. Or it could have been that all day long Finn had been locked up with old people, women whose skin rustled like tracing paper, men whose liver-spotted hands shook as they reached out for another glass of port. Elfine was young and alive. As she raised her lips for his kiss, the worries and darkness of the day seemed momentarily to disappear.

It was a long time before they pulled apart, and only then because they'd both run out of breath.

'We can't go back to the house,' Elfine whispered. 'Not with James padding around.'

She shivered and Finn pulled her towards him once more. It would be romantic, he thought, to run deep into the woods and throw themselves down on a bed of leaves. But it was autumn now and the leaves would be damp and rotting, and with night falling, the air was getting colder. And then a thought occurred to him and he started running in the direction of the castle.

'I'll race you to the garage,' he yelled. With a gleeful

laugh, Elfine was hot on his heels. Once inside the garage Finn and Elfine clambered into the back seat of the car. 'You'll never know how much I've wanted this, Finn,' she whispered, her breath becoming urgent under his touch. 'I've waited all my life for this moment.' And then her words were lost, swallowed up in a frenzy of lust as they found each other.

Afterwards, they untangled their limbs from the constrictions of the narrow seat.

'Elfine——'

She placed a finger on Finn's lips. 'Sh! Don't say anything,' she said. 'Don't apologize, don't try to explain why it happened. Just say you enjoyed it and that will be enough for me.'

Finn kissed her again. 'I think you know I enjoyed it,' he said. 'And from the sounds of it you enjoyed it just as much.'

She smiled coyly.

'But what did you mean when you said you'd waited all your life for this moment? I can't believe you've been thinking of me all this time. You must have had lovers before. What about Connor?'

Elfine threw back her head and laughed. 'Connor!' she said. 'That old fool. He's just persistent, that one. Every now and then I throw a morsel his way. He seems happy enough.'

Finn slid his hand under her shirt. 'You are one foxy lady, Elfine,' he groaned, uncontrollable desire welling up in him once more.

When they left the garage it was dark and their breath ghosted before them as they walked.

'Will you come in for a drink?' Finn asked hopefully.

Elfine shook her head. 'I don't think so, Finn,' she said. 'I think our moment's been and gone.'

'It doesn't have to be,' Finn protested. 'I can stay here longer. Nobody's expecting me back.'

'That's not the impression I got, Finn.'

Finn looked at her questioningly.

'Don't think I didn't notice that girl Carol's eyes on you,' she said.

'Ah, Carol.'

'Don't look at me as if she's someone you met at a party once about five years ago!' Elfine wagged a finger of admonishment at Finn. 'She's in love with you, Finn, surely even you can see that.'

'Carol's just a friend,' Finn protested, conveniently forgetting the speech he'd been about to make to Carol on the ferry. That seemed another world already – so much water had passed under the bridge since then. 'Look, Elfine, I'll stay on. We can get to know each other better, we can––'

'No. Please. We can't, Finn. There are too many differences between us,' Elfine said. 'I belong here and you belong elsewhere. It would never work.'

Finn had to admit – reluctantly – that she might have a point. But that didn't stop him wondering what it would be like to stay here with Elfine just a little while longer.

Elfine stood on tiptoe and kissed him one last time.

'My heart's here, Finn,' she said. 'Just like your grandmother's was. Don't let's spoil what we had by complicating things. Goodnight, my love,' she whispered and turned away from him. 'And goodbye.'

Finn watched her dark silhouette disappear into the night, her frosty breath floating before her on the cold night air. He waited until he could no longer hear the sound of her feet crunching on the gravel that led away from him. Then he turned and headed for the bus.

CHAPTER FIFTEEN

CAROL'S DIARY

January 1st 1998

New year, new diary, new start with Finn – I hope. I'm certain now that Finn fancies me just as much as I fancy him. Nobody forced him to make Beryl roadworthy again, after all. He wouldn't have done it unless he wanted to make me happy. And he did! Seeing Beryl resurrected and reconstructed like that on Christmas Day, with Finn sitting in the driving seat waving up at me was the best Christmas present I've ever had since Mum and Dad got me that signed photo of Jet from the Gladiators when I was in Mrs Newton's class. Now all I have to do is to sit back and wait for him to ask me for a date.

January 11

Today Finn asked me to go to the College Ball with him!!! So who says prayers don't have any effect? I wonder if he'll take me to the Dog first for a drink. It would be nice to show him off. Perhaps I can persuade him to get a haircut and a shave first, so we both look like we're going to the same party. I wonder if he'll try to kiss me and if I'll let him. How far are you supposed to go on a first date, these days? It's been so long that I've forgotten the etiquette.

January 18 1998

Sod it. Sod it. Sod it. I've been unable to write anything at all until just now because I've been too upset. I am positively not speaking to Finn after what happened at the College Ball. That Kate. The tart. Pinching someone's husband isn't enough for that one. Oh, no. She can't get Ruth's Kurt so she makes a play for my boyfriend instead. Turning up to the College Ball in a bright red dress when it's a black and white theme night. How far up herself can that one get? So then she monopolizes Finn all night, leaving me to fend for myself. Well, he's had it. If Finn expects me to forgive him for this, then he's got another thing coming.

24 Jan.

I've decided to forgive him.

25 Jan

He can rot in hell as far as I'm concerned. Kate can have him if she's that desperate. Finn will shag anything and that's a fact. I had almost decided to forgive him for the way he treated me at the College Ball and was on my way over to tell him so. I really wanted to give him the opportunity to put his side of the story. I was prepared to listen to him explain how Kate used her womanly wiles to lure him away from my good influence. It was going to be the reconciliation scene to end all reconciliation scenes.

And then I saw them. He had his arms round her and she was clearly loving every second of it. Then I saw them going into Finn's shed together, still arm in arm. I don't suppose he was giving her a quote for a house clearance. I hope his knob drops off.

Finn couldn't bring himself to read any more, although there was plenty more to be read. Quickly, he tore the extracts from Carol's diary down from the phone box walls where they'd been pasted. Who on earth could have thought it was funny to stick Carol's most intimate thoughts all over the walls of a public telephone box for the whole world to read? he wondered – though he had his suspicions that a jealous and manipulative Kate might be behind it. How many other people had read these pages before him? They wouldn't all be as discreet as him, he could be sure of that.

The poor girl must be going mad with worry, wondering where her diary had got to. It certainly explained what she'd been doing sneaking around the bus earlier on. All this time he'd been away in Ireland and she'd been here in Hollyoaks, she must have thought her diary had been languishing somewhere on the bus where he could have read it any time.

He decided to go and pay Carol a social visit. He would appear nonchalant and casual and in that way he would successfully put her mind at rest. And if that didn't work and she asked him point blank if he'd seen it, he would simply deny it.

CHAPTER SIXTEEN

FINN'S THEORY

'To what do I owe the pleasure?' Carol said, peering round the door at Finn.

She didn't look particularly thrilled to see him, Finn thought, and put it down to the fact that she suspected he'd been rifling through her diary in the wee small hours of the night.

'If you want a drink you'll have to make your own,' she said brusquely. 'I'm watching a film.'

For someone who had sworn undying love in a particularly flowery diary entry, Carol was playing it remarkably cool. Then again, the diary was over a year old. Feelings change. He'd already managed to recover from the broken heart Elfine had left him with, although he knew he'd always have a soft spot for her. Or was it a hard one?

'What you smiling at?' Carol said.

'Oh, so your eyes do leave the screen occasionally, then?'

Carol sniffed and turned up the volume with the remote control.

'I think I've seen this one,' Finn said. 'There's a loony on the loose and he stabs both of them with a kitchen knife but only one of them survives. It's really exciting because we don't know it's the woman who dies until right at the end. She's been written out, you see, 'cos she's got this major part in some Hollywood movie.'

Carol pressed the off button.

'Cheers, Finn,' she said. 'You've saved me the bother of watching the next forty-five minutes.'

'I didn't spoil it for you, did I, Carol? I didn't mean to. I'll get you that coffee, shall I?'

Carol followed him into the kitchen, intrigued as to why he was visiting her. Did he have a guilty conscience? she wondered.

'So,' she asked him, as they sat and sipped their coffee and shared a packet of Hob-Nobs, 'how was Ireland?'

Finn attempted a non-committal look. 'Like you left it, I suppose. Green and damp.'

'And how was Elfine?'

Finn dunked his Hob-Nob a fraction of a second too long and watched half of it fall off into his tea.

'Didn't see much of her,' he said. 'She's got a boyfriend, you know.'

Carol didn't exactly say 'So when's that ever stopped you before?', but Finn could read her like a book. Or like a diary.

What she actually said was, 'Everyone's got a boyfriend. Except me.'

'I haven't got a boyfriend,' Finn said.

Carol stared into her coffee cup and smiled for the first time since Finn had arrived.

'Maybe not,' she said, 'but I bet you could get one any time.'

'What's up, Carol?' Finn was concerned. She seemed really down tonight.

'Oh, nothing,' she said. 'It's just that everyone seems

to be having a wonderful time these days except me. All my life is these days is work.'

Since Carol had lost her job at Parker's, she'd moved on to an equally exhausting profession – working behind the bar at the Dog.

'I wouldn't mind if I made any money,' she continued, 'but once I've paid for the flat and for Beryl, I'm skint. Not that there's anyone to go anywhere with these days, even if I had any money. Everybody but me seems to be paired off.' She yawned loudly. 'Actually, Finn,' she said, 'I'm just tired. Been working long hours. Lack of sleep always makes me a bit depressed.'

Finn took the hint and jumped out of his seat.

'It was nice you popping in like that, anyway,' she said as she opened the door to let him out. 'Sometimes you feel better after a good moan.'

'Nice to know I've got my uses,' he said. 'And seriously, Carol, you know that if there's anything I can do to cheer you up, you only have to say.'

Carol stood on tiptoe and gave Finn a peck on the cheek. 'That's sweet,' she said, then hesitated. 'Er, Finn, can I ask you something?'

'Sure. What is it?'

'It's nothing really,' she said. 'Only I was just wondering. You haven't come across anything of mine in the bus, have you?'

Finn stared at her blankly. 'If I had, you know I would have brought it straight round,' he said.

'Yeah,' Carol said. 'Well, if you do…'

'I'll let you know. Night, Carol.'

'Night, Finn.'

Finn's hand curled round the ball of paper in his jacket pocket. First thing he'd do when he got back was burn this little lot. Or perhaps he'd better read it first, just to make sure his theory was correct. It seemed to him – although this was based on only one reading and really ought to be put through a further test – that in her diary, the only bloke Carol ever mentioned was himself.

CHAPTER SEVENTEEN

A BET

Carol was still moping around, depressed, and Finn and Tony were wondering what they could do to remedy the situation. In spite of all the grief they'd put each other through, the two lads were getting on a lot better these days. Tony was still an officious, pedantic little busy-body, thought Finn, but he had to admit he generally meant well.

'Carol's lost all her sparkle,' Tony remarked. 'Look at the way she's pulling that pint. It's surprising she doesn't get the sack for looking so miserable.'

'Unless Mr Osborne is using her as reverse psychology,' Finn said.

'How do you mean?'

'Well, the more miserable she is, the more miserable the customers feel and the more they drink to drown their sorrows.'

Tony nodded approvingly. 'That's brilliant if it's true,' he said.

'It's Carol's sarcasm I miss,' Finn said gloomily.

Tony agreed. 'It's been a while since she greeted me with those immortal words: "A pint of rattlesnake venom for the gentleman coming up."'

'We're going to have to do something.'

Tony got another couple of pints in while they thought about the Carol problem.

'You see, I think that if someone just asked her out on a date she'd cheer up,' Tony said. 'She's probably just fed up with seeing all her mates with boyfriends while she's still single.'

Occasionally, Finn thought, Tony displayed flashes of wisdom. Only very occasionally, though.

'Is this your considered opinion then, Tony?' he asked.

'Definitely. We could toss a coin. Best of three. The winner gets to ask Carol out on a date. Tails.'

It was heads. Twice. There was no getting away from it. Finn had won. So why wasn't he jumping up and down with joy? He liked Carol, didn't he? Of course he did. But he'd also seen her diary. What if she got the wrong idea and confused a proposal to go out one evening with a proposal of marriage? Once she got the bit between her teeth, he imagined it would be very hard to dislodge. She had all the classic traits of a serious bunny-boiler.

'What's it to be then? A night in the Dog or a romantic dinner for two?' Tony asked.

Finn hardly thought another night in the Dog constituted a night out for someone who spent six nights and six afternoons working there. He liked the idea of a meal. If he ran out of things to say to her, it wouldn't be so noticeable if they were eating at the same time. Carol would simply think Finn's table manners were so impeccable that he never talked with his mouth full.

'I can't do this on my own, though,' he said. 'You'll have to help me, mate.'

Tony looked smug. It wasn't lost on him that Finn only ever addressed him as 'mate' when he wanted something. Tony wasn't inclined to let Finn get his own way so easily this time.

'Nah!' he said. 'Thanks for the offer, mate, but I'm not into threesomes. I shouldn't think Carol would be either.'

Finn grimaced at the thought. 'I wasn't thinking about that side of things, thank you very much. I'm pretty sure I wouldn't come up short in that department. Quite the contrary.'

Tony shifted uncomfortably in his seat. He didn't feel too happy about the way this conversation was going. There'd been a few nasty innuendoes about his own sexual prowess bandied about in the past. It had all settled down again recently, but he was well aware how quickly these things could be stirred up again.

'There is one thing you can do better than anyone I know, though, Tone.'

'Oh?' Tony waited.

Finn sat back in his chair and folded his arms across his chest. He was racking his brains for a way to get Tony to do exactly what he wanted. Flattery generally worked. He decided to give it a go.

'You have a rare talent, Tony,' he began, 'a very rare talent indeed, for creating just the right ambience to put people in a relaxed mood. I wouldn't have a clue how to go about it myself.'

Tony was already beginning to puff his chest out with pride. Finn knew he had him hooked. Now all he had to do was reel in him.

'Nice of you to mention it,' Tony preened. 'I suppose I have been blessed with rather more than my fair share of – how would you describe it, Finn?'

Finn took a hefty swig of his pint, seeking inspiration for the right word.

'I'd say genius, Tony. Mixed with hard-headed organizational skills and a masterly ability to create something from nothing.'

Tony was impressed.

'You could let me loose on that bus of yours if you think that might help,' he suggested. 'I could perhaps do something to change the mood a bit – you know, lighting, heating, that sort of thing.'

Finn nodded. 'I was thinking more about your culinary skills,' he said.

'You'll certainly be on to a winner with Carol if you feed her properly,' Tony agreed. 'That poor girl hasn't a spare ounce of flesh on her. I'll draw up a menu tonight.'

'That's really good of you.' Finn was humble. 'Don't make it too complicated though, will you, Tony. Only I'm no Masterchef.'

'No, but I am,' Tony said, unable and unwilling to keep the pride out of his voice. 'Leave it to me, my friend. All you need to do is provide the wine, the venue, and the scintillating conversation.'

The two of them exchanged big buddy beams. Yup – just like taking candy from a baby, when you know how. Finn smiled to himself.

CHAPTER EIGHTEEN

SOFT LIGHTS, SWEET MUSIC

'This looks lovely, Finn,' Carol said. 'Candles, flowers.' She sniffed approvingly. 'Good food.'

Finn was opening a bottle of wine. 'Just something I knocked up earlier,' he said nonchalantly. Then, realizing how the expression could be misconstrued, he tried to cover it with a nervous laugh. 'Together,' he said. 'I mean "knocked together" not "knocked up".'

'Quite,' Carol said. 'That's something completely different.'

She accepted the glass Finn was holding out to her and took a large gulp.

'Well,' she said. 'Cheers. You shouldn't have gone to all this trouble just for me.'

Finn spoke firmly. 'Carol,' he said. 'I will not hear any more of that sort of talk for the rest of the evening. You are worth just as much consideration and respect as anyone else is.' And he meant it. He couldn't bear the way an attractive, bubbly girl like Carol was always putting herself down.

Carol blushed. She looked quite pretty in the candlelight, Finn thought. Sort of vulnerable and demure and innocent. Very pretty, in fact.

'That's a lovely thing to say, Finn,' she said.

Finn noticed her glass was empty already. Come to think of it, so was his. Must be nerves, he decided, and liberally refilled both their glasses.

'Whoops! No more! You'll have me under the table,' she protested.

Not a bad idea, actually, Finn was beginning to think. He smiled roguishly. 'We should get stuck into this food first, though,' he quipped, then wondered if he'd gone too far.

Carol giggled nervously. 'I don't know why I'm giggling like a fourteen-year-old,' she said. 'I hate girls who giggle. It's just that – well, you know.'

Finn thought he did know. 'We're not used to being so formal, are we?' he said. 'And it's usually you serving me, not the other way round.'

Carol looked briefly displeased to be brought back down to earth, but her expression soon cleared. 'You mean at Parker's,' she said, 'and the Dog? Well this looks much tastier than anything you've been served at any of those places. I didn't know you could cook, Finn.'

Finn refilled their glasses. 'There's a lot you don't know about me, Carol,' he said mysteriously. 'I've been known to turn my hand to a great many things. Now, let me help you to some of this – er – food.'

He really should have asked Tony to explain all the different ingredients of his so-called 'Chef's Salad' but if Carol had noticed he didn't seem to be overly familiar with the contents, she didn't say anything.

It wasn't just the wine that flowed that evening. Finn and Carol found they had a great deal to talk about. Carol told Finn what it was like sharing a house with Tony and Finn sympathized; Finn talked about his stay in Ireland – though he glossed over certain incidents, for obvious reasons – and Carol sympathized. With each exchange of information they slipped more easily into their usual relaxed way of behaving with other.

Halfway through their second bottle of wine, when all the food had been eaten and they were surrounded by debris, Finn noticed that Carol had slipped her shoes off and tucked both her feet up on the seat. She looked so completely at ease that Finn wondered what it might be like to move up closer. He was aware he'd had a bit to drink and might be misreading the signs. But if he was, it was only Carol, after all. She was hardly likely to come over all high and mighty with him.

'Do you remember that little spin you took me for in Beryl that time?' he asked her, inching his way closer with such subtle finesse that he was sure she hadn't even started noticing exactly how close he was getting.

Carol was curling her toes sexily. Finn noticed that her skirt had begun to ride up above her knees in a most attractive manner.

'That was ages ago,' she said, waving away the memory with a dismissive hand. 'I can't remember much about it.'

'Well I can,' Finn said. He placed a hand uncertainly on Carol's knee. Oh no, he suddenly thought, was he moving too fast? To his relief, she left it there. Result.

'You'll have to remind me what happened, then, because it's completely escaped my memory,' Carol said and gave Finn a flirtatious smile.

Finn couldn't believe his luck. She was asking for an action replay. They both moved together at the same time and locked lips.

'I remember there was some confusion about where the gear stick was,' Carol whispered the next time they both came up for air.

Finn gave a muffled moan and closed in on Carol once more. Unfortunately, the plastic seating on the bus left a lot to be desired. It was slippery, for one thing, and the effect of so much friction on it – coupled with the amount of wine they'd already glugged – suddenly propelled Finn and Carol on to the floor. Still locked together in a wrestling embrace that was destined to have only one outcome, the two struggled to get more comfortable.

'Finn, I've just rolled over on to a tomato,' Carol groaned.

'Don't worry about it,' Finn panted. 'There's plenty more in the fridge. Now, what was that suggestion you made earlier about having you under the table?'

'Oh, Finn,' Carol breathed. 'What are we waiting for?'

CHAPTER NINETEEN

ENOUGH IS AS GOOD AS A FEAST

'So it went OK then?'

Tony was fishing for information. Finn decided to let him angle. No point in making things easy for him.

'Lovely food, Tony. The salad dressing in particular was exactly to Carol's taste. Piquant, I think, is the word you chefs would employ.'

Tony looked miffed. 'I think the least you owe me is a detailed account of your date with Carol after all the trouble I went to with that food,' he said.

'A gentleman never kisses and tells, Tony, surely you know that,' Finn replied, enjoying Tony's frustration. 'Suffice it to say we both enjoyed ourselves very much and have repeated the experience on numerous occasions since.'

Tony's mouth dropped open. 'On the bus?' he asked.

'Well it's hardly the season for doing it in the open air,' Finn said.

He and Carol had been having a ball since their dinner party and it was looking highly likely that their shagging marathon was set to run and run. For a petite girl, Carol had an unexpected amount of stamina.

Finn was concerned that she might wear him out before long. Still, it would be a pleasant way to go.

He'd been surprised and not a little pleased at the boundless enthusiasm Carol had shown for sex. Perhaps it was the result of all those months of pent-up passion. But he was beginning to feel like a kid with a sweet tooth who'd just landed a job at Thornton's. The initial thrill of being told you could have as much chocolate as you wanted might very quickly begin to pall. It was definitely possible to have too much of a good thing. And Carol was most certainly that.

Only this morning, he'd sneaked on to the bus for forty winks after a particularly gymnastic session the previous night. This had been combined with an early morning wake-up call the like of which he'd never experienced in his wildest dreams. He had been roused – in more ways than one – by Carol climbing all over him.

The resulting shenanigans had left him late for an appointment with a contact of his who did a nice line in Hallowe'en masks and who Finn had in mind to supply costumes for the college Hallowe'en Ball. Well, it couldn't be helped, he supposed. He hadn't exactly put up a fight. Mind you, he was so tired now that he was beginning to wish he had.

He searched around in his pocket for a scrap of paper that might have the contact's number on it, but it was impossible to locate among the sweet wrappers and chocolate bars that cluttered the pocket. Carol had taken to stocking him up with high-calorie snacks to provide him with the energy she clearly thought he needed to keep up with her. Perhaps he'd better have a Mars bar now, just in case Carol put in another appearance before tonight.

'Well, if you ask me, mate, you look totally shagged out,' Tony said. 'You could do with a holiday.' He puffed himself up self-importantly. 'Actually, Lucy and I are off on a mini-break ourselves this very weekend.'

Finn's ears pricked up. Tony, if he wasn't much mistaken, had a double bed, about the only object belonging to him that Finn could honestly say he had ever coveted. Perhaps he was getting old, but sex in a double bed was beginning to seem like a much more attractive prospect these days than sex in the narrow bed he shared with Carol.

It wasn't just the sex, though. The more he thought about it, the more he convinced himself that a post-coital snooze would give him much more energy to carry on than Carol's chocolate bars ever would. All they were doing was giving him tooth decay. He suddenly perked up.

'Don't even think about it,' Tony said. 'My bed is off limits.'

'My good man, I have no idea what you're talking about,' Finn lied.

Tony drew himself up to his full height and attempted to threaten Finn with a menacing stare. 'If I find out you've been sleeping in my bed when I get back,' he said, 'I'll rip your balls off and pan-fry them in garlic butter.'

Finn noticed Carol striding across the yard towards him. She was wearing an expression he had begun to recognize – and fear.

'Have you got half an hour, Finn?' she asked sweetly. 'Only I'm on my break and I thought we could... Oh, hello, Tony.'

Finn gulped. 'Lovely to see you, Carol,' he said. 'You go on up and make yourself comfy. Give me a moment and I'll be all yours.'

To Tony he hissed the words: 'You'll have to sew them back on first,' before he boarded the bus and mounted the stairs wearily.

CHAPTER TWENTY

THE MEMORY LINGERS ON

As suddenly as it started, it was all over. Finn couldn't believe it. How could it have gone so wrong between him and Carol? Happy memories replayed in his head like the closing sequence to a Jamie Oliver cookery programme. Brilliant times, food and fun and fabulous frolics, air-brushed to perfection. Pukka.

Tony's bed. What a laugh that had been. Carol in the bathroom slipping into something more comfortable while he fiddled about with the nuts and bolts. All he'd wanted was to see if he could work out whether it was possible to dismantle the bed he coveted so much and transport it on to the bus. Then Carol had made a dramatic entrance, leapt on to the bed and it had collapsed beneath them. They'd laughed so much after the initial shock it had been worth the look on Tony's face. Memory number one.

Memory number two: that squirty cream fight. Carol had started it. Finn grinned at the memory. Mad. Passionate. Wonderful. Even now he could feel her moist tongue as it slid over his body, licking away the whorls of cream, then falling upon him with unrestrained lust. Which he had returned. Generously.

It wasn't fair. Just because of something he'd said. Under duress. Bloody Geri. Bloody blonde, bloody rich, bloody student. He could murder her. She was a Jude type. Voluptuous. The type to say, 'We're having a bit of a party, why don't you step inside for an hour?'

And he was the type to say, 'Oh, well, if it's only for an hour I'm sure Carol won't mind.' And Carol, of course, was the type that Finn had gone through life feeling obliged to keep in the dark about any of his extra-curricular activities. There was no reason at all for Carol to find out he'd spent a bit of time with another girl, he'd stupidly thought. No reason at all. Good old Carol. Even if she did find out, she wouldn't mind.

Only she'd minded very much when Geri let slip exactly how she knew Finn and Tony's little secret. When it came out at the Bonfire Party that Tony and Finn had had a bet on to ask her for a date, Carol, unfortunately, had not followed the script. She hadn't said, 'Oh, silly me. Fancy me thinking you really liked me, Finn. Fancy me thinking you really respected me. I see it now, you were only having a laugh.'

No. She'd been hurt. Deeply hurt. She'd fled the party in floods of tears and he hadn't seen her since. Occasionally he'd caught a glimpse of her shadow before it shrank away against a wall. Finn despised himself more than he despised Geri, who was only conforming to type. Why did he always fall for it when women said 'You can tell me, I won't tell anyone'?

And why, when things were going well with a girl, did he always have to go and mess it up? He just couldn't resist playing up to the advances of a fit blonde, and there was always a little corner of him that fancied himself as the roguish, love 'em and leave 'em type. Maybe there was more of his dad in him than he'd care to admit.

Finn was cleaning up the shed. Cleaning up the shed was something he did whenever life decided to kick him in the arse. Thankfully, it didn't happen too often. There were things in here he hadn't seen for months. That cable he'd rigged from Tony's electricity supply. A bunch of old newspapers. A child's stair gate, though he didn't have a clue how that had found its way in there. Two hours later the shed was ship-shape. Finn needed a drink.

Unfortunately, it wasn't Carol's night off. She had perfected this way of ignoring him that made him feel the most singled-out man in the room. Finn decided to get drunk. It was a coward's way out, but the only way he knew to cope with a situation that was deeply upsetting him.

At closing time he plucked up the courage to approach her.

'Carol,' he slurred, 'I am prepared to beg. Take me back. Please. I love you.'

Carol's sneer made him feel the size of an ant.

'Read my lips, Finn. Piss off!' Carol said, direct and to the point as usual.

Finn protested. 'How can you be so cruel, Carol? We were so good together. I never meant for it to go pear-shaped like this.'

Carol wasn't prepared to give an inch. She was in her stride now. 'What did people say before they said "pear-shaped"?' she asked him.

Finn shrugged. 'I don't know,' he said. 'Carol, please. I'm begging.'

'Next.' She turned away from him and put on a bright smile for the next customer.

When she turned back to him, it wasn't to resume their conversation but to remove his empty glass. He might as well not have been there.

Finn said: 'Wrong.'

'I beg your pardon?' Carol said, as though they were talking long distance.

'I think people would have probably said that things had gone wrong. Before they said pear-shaped.'

Carol smiled a harsh, cold, brief smile. 'Simple, but effective,' she said. 'And do you know what, Finn? They would have been right.'

CHAPTER TWENTY-ONE

AN OLD COWBOY NEVER FORGETS

Finn had never felt so low. Carol was still refusing to speak to him and he had no idea what he could do to change her mind. The situation seemed utterly hopeless.

'The only way to get over one woman is to get on top of another,' Lewis advised him.

'Ha, ha, very funny,' Finn said, unamused. They'd been talking about going for a drink, but like every other conversation Finn had these days, it wasn't long before the subject turned back to Carol.

'That Geri's got the hots for you,' Lewis continued. 'The way she's been hanging round your bus lately, you'd be a fool not to invite her on board.'

'She's already invited herself,' Finn admitted grudgingly. 'Only I don't want her. I only want Carol.'

Lewis made one last attempt at being a sympathetic listener. He couldn't believe what had got into Finn. All this stuff with Carol had gone on far too long, he thought, but then again, a mate was a mate.

'Women, eh?' he said.

'Can't live with them, can't live with them,' Finn said gloomily.

Finn – the kind of bloke who could
charm the birds out of the trees,
or at least out of their clothes.

Carol and Finn – the only man she
mentioned in her diary was him.

Another business venture up the spout!

Finn, Lewis and their Roman visitor.

Lord Kildiggin and his castle.

Finn and Elfine – childhood sweethearts...

...and what Carol doesn't know can't hurt her.

Finn baling out on Carol – not for the last time.

This behaviour's enough to put anyone off their breakfast.

Lewis and Finn – business partners through thick and thin.

Finn and Victoria – will it all work out?

Lewis rolled his eyes in sheer irritation at Finn's self-pitying mood, before deciding to slope off to the Dog on his own. Anybody's company would be better than Finn's, he decided.

'I'll leave you to enjoy your misery in peace then,' he said.

Finn nodded. 'See you, mate. Lewis's sarcasm was completely lost on him.

He was still leaning up against the side of the bus, staring dreamily into space, when Tony arrived.

'Lovely day,' Tony said.

Finn nodded. 'Makes you wish you were glad to be alive,' he said.

Tony sighed. 'Not Carol again,' he said. 'You not over her yet? Face it, Finn, you and her are history. I've seen what she's done to all the photos she took that had you on them,' he added. 'And put it this way, in the future, when she's a little old lady with grandchildren, they will have no idea what you look like.'

'I wouldn't blame her for cutting me out of them,' Finn said. 'She's already cut me out of her life.'

Only that morning she'd cut him dead when their paths had crossed. She'd been coming out of the Drive 'n' Buy and he'd been going in. It had felt just as if she'd stuck a knife in his guts and twisted it round and round again.

'Look, mate,' Tony began. 'You've heard the saying: when one door closes, another door opens. Geri's been asking after you. Why don't you pop round? Ask her over for a meal? Ply her with wine. You know, exactly like you did with Carol.'

'Thanks, Tony. I'll think about it,' Finn said. 'Now if you don't mind, I've got work to do.'

Tony said goodbye and moved on, leaving Finn to turn over his advice. Fact number one: Carol had dumped him. Fact number two: Geri fancied him rotten and had made that clear on more than one occasion. Fact number three: Carol had seen Geri getting off his bus and decided, quite wrongly as it happened, that the two of them had ended up doing the two-consenting-adults bit. Whereas in reality they'd been discussing Carol, and how she'd broken Finn's heart.

Finn sighed. He couldn't wander around mooning over Carol and behaving like a lovesick sap for ever. She was obviously having none of it. However hard he tried to remedy the situation, he knew that Carol was firmly resolved to give him no more chances. She expected the worst from him. So what was the point of disappointing her by continuing to ignore Geri's advances? Finn decided his logic was irrefutable. He would invite Geri round that very evening.

He rarely remembered anything his father had told him, but he remembered this: the only way to get your nerve back once you've fallen off your horse is to get straight back in the saddle. Better start polishing up your spurs then, Finn, he told himself.

CHAPTER TWENTY-TWO

DEAR CAROL, LOVE FINN

Dear Carol,

I hope you are fully recovered from the events of Millennium Eve.

Finn screwed that one up and threw it in the bin.

Dear Carol,

How are you? How's your little dog? Meryl, I think you decided to call her.

This one he made into a dart and aimed it successfully out of the window. Carol knew crap when she read it.

Dear Carol,

Ireland is much the same. Full of shamrocks and blarney, which is the Irish word for bullshit. James the butler sends his love. As does Elfine. Did I tell you she was engaged? To no less than Dr Connor O'Brien. They seem very happy. Or so James says. He has a thing going with Dr O'Brien's cleaning lady so if anyone knows, she should.

I haven't seen anything of either of them, myself. Too busy sorting out the estate. And somewhere to live for myself when I get back to Hollyoaks, of course, now that the bus is a charred ruin.

No good. Too self-pitying. Why should she care if he was homeless?

Dear Carol,
Perhaps we can make a new start in the new millennium. The next thousand years can't possibly be as bad as the last as far as our romance is concerned.

Too clever-clever. Why couldn't he just write the truth?

Dear Carol
I've bought a river boat to live on – a step up the property ladder from a double-decker bus, wouldn't you say? And if ever it catches fire, there will always be water at hand to put out the flames.
Carol, I bought my houseboat with you in mind. I have dreams of leading you by the arm and down the steps. This is my cooking area, I'll say. And here is where I eat. If you look at me the way you've looked at me on lucky occasions in the past, I'll even be able to show you my sleeping quarters. There's a toilet too. Not the flushing kind, the chemical sort, but it's a step up from a hole in the bottom of the boat – just.

Finn put down his pen for a moment, then wrote some more.

You have every right to be angry with me after Geri and everything. After the fire I only made it worse by

– 84 –

pretending to be hurt much more seriously than I actually was. But ask yourself why, Carol. Just ask yourself why. When the bus exploded, and you and I got separated in the confusion that followed, I was worried sick. Where were you?

That's all I could think of. When you appeared out of the blue that like, all tender concern, OK, so I milked it for all it was worth. You stroking my brow and feeding me sips of water so tenderly. Well, Carol, it was my dream. Especially since you'd been ignoring me for weeks on end.

Finn read through this last attempt. It was no good. He couldn't send it. Suppose it got into the wrong hands? He tore it up and began again.

Hey, Babe.

No. Absolutely not. This last effort would positively be his last.

Dear Carol,
Weather is here. Wish you and I were fine. Back soon.
                                        Love Finn.

CHAPTER TWENTY-THREE

DEAR FINN, LOVE CAROL

Dear Finn

I hope you get this letter. There can't be that many Kildiggin Castles in Kildiggin. Tony told me you'd gone back to Ireland for a bit to sort something out. I suppose that now you're a lord you've got lots of stuff to see to. For a start there'll be all those peasants in need of a good flogging for poaching your pheasants – or is the spelling the other way round? And no doubt there'll be a few old ladies to check out on suspicion of practising sorcery – take my advice, if they drown when you throw them in the river, they're witches – dead ones. All this will leave you very little time for wenching and whoring, but knowing you, you'll fit it in somewhere in your busy schedule.

Finn, when I thought you were trapped on that bus and you were going to roast alive, I realized how much I loved you. There, now I've said it. I remember watching it go up in flames and thinking that if you died, my life wouldn't be worth living. I thought of all the horrible things I'd said to you and the number of times I'd turned you away when you told me that you were sorry for hurting you and taken you in my arms and hugged you. Because, you see, on Millennium Eve, I thought that I'd never get the chance again.

I believe now that I went through mental agony that night. When you popped up next day, large as life and twice as natural, why didn't I throw myself at you and say let's start again? Well, I honestly don't know, Finn. We all do things we can't account for, don't we? Maybe I was punishing you for making me worry myself sick about you. Or maybe it was because you lied to me by pretending you were really hurt and all you had was a few cuts and bruises. That was contemptible, Finn, even for you, you have to agree.

I should have left it there – left us and our relationship firmly in the past, I mean. But you see, Finn, I can't help but keep coming back to the fact that I love you. And because I love you, I forgive you. What you and Tony did, having that bet to see which one would have the pleasure of taking me out, was just a schoolboy prank, I see that now. It may have started out a laugh for you, but I believe you when you said that after a while it turned into something else for you.

And I believe you about Geri, and about Kate and about Kerri. Girls will always throw themselves at your feet, Finn. And do you know why? It's not for your suave good looks and your sophisticated line in patter. It's not even because you can get them cheap knickers and tights from Ali the Turk. It's because basically you don't care anything about them and that makes them care about you more.

So, while you drift through relationships – ringing or not ringing, being faithful or not being faithful – there is some poor girl on the other end of the phone biting her nails down to the knuckles and eaten up with love for you.

A word of advice from your Aunty Carol, though, Finn. One day the tables will be turned and you will be the one left with the broken heart. It may not happen soon, but it will happen, because your karma always catches up with you in the end.

Well, that brings me back to us. We left things dangling a bit when you left to go to Ireland. When you get back you might decide that all in all I'm not worth the bother, as I only seem to want to change you and reform you. I wouldn't blame you, although I'd be sorry. Finn, you know where I live. Come and knock on my door and tell me you're back. This time I won't turn you away.

Carol

Carol sealed the envelope with a sigh and picked up her jacket: The clock on the wall said 5.40. If she ran, she'd get the last post and Finn would be reading this letter with his kedgeree and buttered crumpets or whatever it was the gentry had for their breakfasts.

The postman was already there when she reached the corner. He was on his knees, unlocking the postbox and tipping the mail into his sack. She held back and watched him as he worked. He looked up and saw her.

'Want me to take that, love?' he asked. 'Only I haven't got all day.'

Carol thought about it. She did, didn't she? Then why didn't she just give him the letter.

'Er,' she said. She checked the envelope again, as if searching for an answer for her dilemma. 'I'm not sure.'

'Well, make up your mind, darling,' the postman said. 'I've got other postboxes to empty.' He held out his hand in a businesslike manner. 'Yes or no?'

'No,' Carol said at last and turned on her heels. 'I've changed my mind.'

As she ran down the street she ripped the letter into a thousand tiny pieces and scattered it like confetti behind her.

CHAPTER TWENTY-FOUR

MERYL

The world was divided into two sorts of people, so they said: cat lovers and dog lovers. Finn had never really liked dogs, so he guessed he was in the former camp, although he didn't really like cats either, ever since his grandma's old tabby, Daisy, had scratched his arm and drawn blood when he was a boy.

He had nothing against proper dogs – farm dogs, sheep dogs, those cute mountain rescue dogs with flagons of beer round their necks, and like most people he'd own up to a sneaking respect for guide dogs. He even tolerated police dogs, just.

But he'd never seen the point of poodles. All his instincts told him that they were mean-spirited, spiteful little critters with very little intelligence and absolutely no sense of humour. Since making Meryl's acquaintance, he had been proven right again and again.

Trouble was, Finn loved Carol and Carol loved Meryl and if Finn wanted to get Carol back, then he'd have to tolerate her pooch. While he'd been away in Ireland, Meryl had replaced him in Carol's affections and obviously the little mutt was reluctant to give up its number one position in Carol's heart and Carol's bed. It hadn't taken Finn long to work out that Meryl and himself were rivals. How could they hope to live side by side amicably when Meryl hated Finn as much as he hated her?

At the beginning he did try to be friendly. But whenever he addressed her by name, Meryl bared her teeth and once, when Finn made the mistake of trying to stroke her, she leapt up at him and almost knocked him over.

'You've just got to be patient, Finn,' Carol told him time and time again. 'She's just nervous of men, that's all. She's probably had a few bad experiences with them. You can't blame her for not being a pushover.'

Since Finn and Carol had got back together, Finn sensed that everything she said had a double meaning. It was not only Meryl whose paws had been burned by some nasty man, was the implication of Carol's words. So watch it and don't try any funny business with me ever again, was the implied warning. Finn wondered when he would be fully forgiven for his past misdemeanours, if ever.

But if it meant keeping close to Carol until she had regained her confidence in him, Finn would have been prepared to share Carol with a herd of elephants – though getting them all on to his barge might have been tricky. At least Meryl was small enough to be ignored – a fact that more than once had sent him sprawling across the floor, clutching his gnawed ankle in agony while Meryl limped for refuge into Carol's arms, yelping pitifully.

Both Carol and Meryl had spent the rest of the night glowering malevolently at Finn – to whom they'd assigned the role of villain and not victim, and thus totally undeserving of their sympathy.

For all the aggravation, though, Finn was determined that this time Carol should know that he meant business.

He was falling over himself to prove to her that he had turned over a new leaf, even going so far as to commission a portrait of her, which he presented to her with a speech in which he swore his undying love. It had worked. That night she stayed with him on the boat and never once complained of leaks or draughts or water rats.

True enough, she'd have been well within her rights to complain of all three. A lesser woman would have abandoned ship at the first hint of a leak. But Carol was a trouper, and in his heart Finn knew that it was for that reason that he was prepared to jump through hoops to win her back.

'You're hard work, Carol,' he told her one night when they were tucked up in bed, safe from the storms outside and jealously guarded by Meryl, who yelped each time Finn moved his feet.

'Well, maybe I am,' Carol replied, suddenly full of her old spirit. 'But I'm worth it. And you love it.'

Finn had to admit he did, and would have loved to show her exactly how much, but Meryl snarled at him from the end of the bed, which rather put a damper on his passion.

'It's going really well these days, isn't it, between you me?' Carol said a few days later. 'It's not all that bad living on a leaky boat. Once you get used to the toilet arrangements and the lack of washing facilities.'

'And it's only a matter of time before she's berthed in dry dock at Hollyoaks and I can carry out some repairs,' Finn said.

'Everything's looking up then,' Carol said.

'Yeah, I think you're right, Carol. I think you're right,' Finn said.

Finn had seen enough disaster movies to know that the day it was acknowledged that things were going well was the day the bomb exploded, leaving the hero blind and limbless, and the heroine discovered she had an inoperable brain tumour as well as losing both parents in a plane crash. He should have guessed that disaster was round the corner.

CHAPTER TWENTY-FIVE

BAILING OUT

'Finn! Finn! Wake up, for God's sake! The boat's leaking.'

Carol shook Finn until he was forced to abandon his dream-world harem of Anna Friel, Gail Porter and Denise van Outen in his luxury beach home in Malibu and return to real life.

'See you later, girls,' he whispered sadly, in fond farewell.

'Finn! There's water everywhere!' Carol screamed and leapt on to the bed for safety. 'I'm getting out before I drown. Grab Meryl. Quick, move!'

In a flash Finn was wide awake, wondering what on earth to do. He looked round for a couple of buckets and a pair of wellies. Of course, there were never any around when you needed them.

The most vital thing, he decided, was to calm Carol down. She was beginning to transfer her hysteria to Meryl. In fact, it was hard to decide which of the two was making the most racket. He clambered aboard the bed to join Carol.

'Don't panic!' he shouted. 'Don't panic!'

Carol gave him an irritable little push.

'For God's sake, Finn! Stop all that Captain Mainwaring stuff and find something to bail us out with,' she said through gritted teeth. 'Why ever did I let you persuade me to come and live on this…this…colander?'

In spite of there being more important matters to consider – such as drowning – this comment hurt Finn's feelings. He'd been under the impression that Carol had come aboard of her own free will and now she was talking as if he'd twisted her arm. Anyway, they'd discuss that later. Bailing out the boat was the main priority at this moment.

'It's not a bad leak, Carol,' he said. He couldn't find a bucket but he had managed to lay his hands on a couple of saucepans. 'See, the water level's going down really quickly.'

Carol glowered at him. 'What was your last job?' she asked him. 'Publicity agent for the *Titanic*? It's all right, Meryl.'

Meryl, who was yelping piteously in Carol's arms, gazed up at her trustingly. Why can't Carol look at me like that once in a while? thought Finn. He had a sudden bright idea. It involved getting this boat out of the water pronto.

'I think even Meryl could have worked that one out, Finn,' Carol said.

'No, listen.' He struggled to make himself heard above Meryl's whining.

'I'm listening, Einstein,' Carol said. 'It'd better be good.'

'We'll tow the boat along the boat path behind Beryl and try and pull her to the Dog.'

Carol bailed even more frantically.

'Who's this "we"?' she asked him.

Finn suspected he had a mutiny on his hands. Drastic measures were called for. He silently swore that if that bloody Meryl didn't shut up, he'd pitch her over the side any second now.

'There, there, Meryl,' he simpered, catching Carol catching him glaring at the dog. 'We'll soon have you safe and dry.'

'What do you want me to do, then?'

Finn felt a rush of love and gratitude to Carol. 'Carol,' he said, 'you're an absolute legend.'

'I don't want to be a legend,' she said. 'I'm only nineteen. Only dead people are legends. Now tell me what to do.'

Patiently, Finn explained that he was going to off-load Beryl from the back of the boat and tether the boat to the car. Obviously, this necessitated Carol bailing while he did so.

'What are we going to do with Meryl while all this is going on?'

Finn restrained himself from telling her what he'd like to do with the pesky poodle and said instead that she'd have to be tied up on the bank.

'You can't do that to Meryl!' Carol shouted. 'It would be cruel!'

'So you'd rather she drowned, then?' Finn asked.

Carol was forced to see the sense of Finn's argument.

'OK,' she said grudgingly, 'if it'll get us out of here.'

'Trust me,' Finn said, as he went about his next task. 'I'll have this boat in dry dock in a jiffy.'

CHAPTER TWENTY-SIX

SCUPPERED!

Some time later, the boat and Finn, with Carol at the wheel of Beryl, drew to a halt outside the Dog. Neither Carol nor Finn could decide what they wanted first – a drink or a pee.

'It wasn't so bad, was it?' Finn said later, after both necessities had been dealt with.

'Don't speak to me,' Carol said. 'I've never been so wet and miserable in my life. And you nearly killed my dog.'

Inwardly, Carol was congratulating herself for never having sent Finn that love letter.

'I didn't nearly kill your dog, Carol,' Finn said. 'I just – lost her for a few minutes.'

Pulling the weight of an entire houseboat had been one load too many for Beryl's sewing machine of an engine to cope with. She'd broken down on numerous occasions on the journey. Several times, Finn was forced to have a look at the engine and see if he could coax it back to life, while Carol sat inside the car, cracking her finger joints menacingly and staring grimly straight ahead.

It must have been during one of Finn's investigations that Meryl had dived for cover inside the engine. Finn had replaced the bonnet without thinking, and poor Meryl would have been dead now if Carol hadn't forced him to look for her there as a last resort. Her reasoning had been that she had to be somewhere and looking for her in the car engine was a better alternative than getting the lifeguards out to drag her from the water. Privately, Finn didn't think the lifeguards would have come out for an annoying little mutt, but he had learned that there was a time to speak and a time to remain silent.

Back in the Dog, Carol expressed an overwhelming desire for a wash.

'Then have one,' Finn said. 'We both can. They do have ladies' and gents' bogs with hot running water, soap and towels here, remember?'

Carol's expression glazed over. 'Hot running water, soap and towels,' she repeated, as if Finn was describing a gourmet three-course meal he'd once had and she hadn't eaten for a month.

'Come on, Finn,' she said. 'I'll see you outside by the boat.'

Finn was happily scrubbing his nails when Mr Osborne, the landlord, popped his head round the door. He was irate when he saw Finn's clothes all over the floor and his half-naked body at the sink.

'What the bloody hell do you think you're doing?' he shouted. 'I'll have no tramps on my premises.'

Finn had had enough trouble that night to last him a lifetime. He grabbed his clothes and haphazardly threw them on as he hobbled out of the toilets, Mr Osborne pursuing him angrily off the premises.

'Clear off, before I call the police!' he yelled.

Carol was waiting for him outside. She looked cleaner, but it hadn't made her any happier.

'I can't find the boat,' she said. 'I've walked up and down this stretch of the river but I just can't seem to see it anywhere.'

Finn buried his head in his hands. Only Carol could think you could lose a boat. And only Carol could refer to a boat as 'it'.

'She's sunk, Carol,' he said, wondering if this would be the first time Carol had ever seen him cry.

Carol's smile was a nervous one. 'You know,' she said, 'I was just starting to suspect that's what had happened.'

CHAPTER TWENTY-SEVEN

SUSPICION

Since the boat had gone down, things seemed to have taken a leap backwards. Once again, Carol was living at Tony's, and once again, she was having doubts about Finn. She couldn't quite put her finger on it but she knew he was up to something. He was keeping something from her. She decided to confront him the next time he called round.

Finn had been staying at Lewis and Ruth's since the houseboat's suicide by drowning. At the time he'd made some wisecrack about the boat deciding death was a better way out than having to live with Meryl, but Carol hadn't even smiled. Well, she'd bared her teeth. So had Meryl.

It saddened Carol to think that those two still weren't getting on. She'd thought about family therapy, but hadn't yet found the right opportunity to broach the subject. She tried to pinpoint the moment when she'd first started to suspect Finn wasn't living up to the promises he'd made her the last time he'd done the dirty on her.

There was the time he'd told her he had an appointment at the bank, for a start. She should have realized then that there was something going on. Finn didn't do banks. He did scribbling on the back of an envelope and scratching behind the ear. But not banks.

There were also those other excuses. 'I'm just popping out to see Lewis,' had been his favourite. Carol began to count up the number of times Finn had given her some half-assed excuse about business meetings with Lewis and the exhausted look he'd had on his return. So he thought he could put one over on her again, did he?

'You bastard!' Carol breathed as she looked out of her window for Finn. 'You slimy toe-rag.'

The moment the words were out, Carol regretted them. This was no way to carry on a relationship. After the fire, hadn't she decided that Finn was too important to lose? Trust was the name of the game she'd settled on. But all the same…

'Only me.'

Carol jumped. Finn must have been knocking for ages. He looked knackered, Carol thought – the image of a man who'd been up to something he shouldn't be. She was beginning to doubt the wisdom of spending a week's wages on a Valentine's present and card for him – not to mention the wrapping paper, although she could always find a use for that, she guessed.

But Valentine presents worked both ways. Perhaps she should leave the cross-examination until February the fifteenth. It would be awful if he'd spent a load of money on a romantic weekend trip to Paris and she told him they were finished before she'd even set foot on the train. Even as the thought popped into her mind, Carol despised herself for being so materialistic.

She drew a deep breath and came out with it.

'What's going on, Finn?' She'd meant to be subtle, but this was too important for that. 'If there's somebody else, you only have to say. As long as you realize that I'll beat your brains out if I find out you've been lying to me.'

Finn sank into Carol's best armchair and closed his eyes, exhausted.

'What am I being accused of now?' he demanded. 'All I've done all day is try to keep out of Ruth's way and clean up the yard.'

Carol hovered, small and determined, waiting for Finn to give himself away.

'So you've got nothing to tell me then?' she demanded.

Finn hadn't a clue what Carol was going on about. He'd come here for a bit of peace and quiet. He'd always suspected he was a bit of a hermit by nature and living with Ruth and Lewis was making him surer by the minute. Carol, at least, understood his need for a stress-free environment – or so he'd been thinking on his way over here. But it seemed he was wrong.

'Something's different, Finn,' Carol said. 'I know you're keeping a secret from me.'

Finn looked at her, puzzled. 'I'm not keeping anything from you, Carol,' he said. 'Honest.'

Carol still didn't trust herself to believe him. 'So you're not seeing another woman, then?'

Finn gaped at her. The idea was preposterous.

'Carol!' he exclaimed. 'For a start, where would I get the energy for another woman after I've done a day at the yard? And where would I take her? I can just see Ruth's face.'

Carol thought about this. 'So you really haven't got anything to tell me, then?'

How many opportunities to worm his way out of a tricky situation was a woman supposed to give the man she loved? she wondered. She was coming perilously close to running out of goodwill here.

'Finn,' she said, patiently, 'I'll give you a clue. Remember that suit I found inside that Top Man bag? And that smart shirt?'

Finn's face cleared. 'Oh, that,' he said. 'Is that all you're worried about?'

Carol started to relax, but not too much. You couldn't take anything for granted with Finn.

CHAPTER TWENTY-EIGHT

ST VALENTINE'S DAY MASSACRE

'So she's forgiven you, then?'

Lewis and Finn were clearing up the yard.

'Nothing to forgive, mate.' Finn had to shout to make himself heard. He was mixing cement for a new wall, a task that took him back to making mud pies during school break.

'You should have told Carol from the first about wanting to buy the yard and the trouble we had trying to raise the money,' Lewis said. 'Ruth and I always talk problems over. You know what they say – a problem shared is a problem halved.'

Finn thought about this. More like a problem shared was a problem doubled.

'I didn't want to burden Carol any more than I had to,' he said. 'What if I'd built her hopes up about getting the bank loan for the yard and then it had all gone pear-shaped?'

'I suppose so,' Lewis said. 'But it's not surprising she started suspecting you of two-timing her when she found the suit you'd hidden for your visit to the bank manager. She must have thought you'd got a posh date with another girl.'

'Not to mention the look on my face every time I came back from talking money – or the lack of it – with you,' he said. 'Anyway, it's sorted now. We've got the yard and Carol's still madly in love with me.'

'So where are you taking her Valentine's Day?'

Finn felt the colour drain from his face. Lewis looked at him.

'You've forgotten, haven't you?' he said.

It took the rest of the morning plus the price of a pint and a cheese sandwich at the Dog to persuade Lewis to change his reservation for dinner for two at Deva to dinner for four.

'But you owe me one, Finn,' he said. 'And I'm telling you now that for this it'll be a big one.'

Carol was delighted at the prospect of a meal out, though not so sure about sharing a table with Lewis and Ruth. But after Finn explained it was as much a celebration of finally securing the yard as a Valentine's Day thing, she went along with it.

'Just don't be late picking me up, that's all,' she warned Finn when he gave her the news.

* * *

February the fourteenth dawned cloudy and overcast. To Finn it was just another day. He had a lot to do and the prospect of having to work outside in the cold and rain didn't please him much.

Mr Morgan had made them promise that if he sold them the yard, the deal was to clear it of all the rubbish they'd accumulated over the past year. They'd agreed enthusiastically enough at the time but the reality was long hours and aching limbs. And dirt. Lots of it.

Finn worked hard all day and when neither his back nor his limbs could take any more punishment, he decided to pack it in. A nice long soak with Carol scrubbing his back was what he wanted most, followed by a takeaway and an early night.

It was while he was on his way to Carol's, mentally tossing up between the comparative merits of a number twenty-five and a number thirty-two, that he realized he'd made completely different arrangements for this evening. In twenty minutes precisely, he and Carol were meant to be sharing a candlelit supper for four with Lewis and Ruth at Deva.

He sprinted the last few yards, mentally preparing himself for the torrent of wrath he knew would descend on him as soon as Carol opened the door.

'Where the flippin' 'eck have you been till this time?' she fumed. 'And what do you look like? If you think I'm going out to a restaurant with you looking like that, you've got another think coming.'

Finn didn't think this was the moment to compliment Carol on her own appearance.

'Give me the keys to the van,' she snapped. 'I'll wait ten minutes max. You know where the bath is. Have one. And make sure Meryl's settled before you leave.'

Then she was gone, in a cloud of the CK1 she'd bought Finn for Christmas.

As he ran the bath water, Finn could have sworn that Meryl was laughing at him. That dog took pleasure from his discomfort, he was sure.

'What you looking at?' he sneered. 'Never seen one of these before?'

Meryl chose to ignore him and turned away in order to lick her bottom.

What happened next, after Finn had quickly dried and dressed himself, briefly introduced a comb to his hair (they didn't hit it off), and let himself out of Carol's flat, was the work of moments. But nothing, after this, would ever be the same again.

Finn couldn't have known this fact, otherwise he wouldn't have whistled so cheerfully under his breath as he let himself out. He wouldn't have pretended that he hadn't glimpsed Meryl slip out into the dark, in his wake. He wouldn't have decided that it was better to ignore this fact if he wanted to get to the restaurant before it closed. When Carol asked him if Meryl was all right, he wouldn't have replied: 'All tucked up and fast asleep.'

Worst of all, he wouldn't have been gripped by a feeling of nausea when he put the van into reverse and rolled backwards into something soft. Finn knew immediately that he'd hit Meryl, who had decided that a leisurely pace would give her ample time to get out of the way of Finn's car, having seen the number of manoeuvres he usually took to turn the car round to face the other way.

She'd never been wrong before, but sadly poor Meryl's judgement that night was woefully wide of the mark. This time, Finn managed to turn the car round in just three moves. And that was one move too many for Meryl.

AUNTY VI

Carol's growing disappointment as each new day failed to bring any news of Meryl, dead or alive, was making Finn sicker by the minute, because he knew that the longer he left it, the more impossible it was for him to own up to what he'd done. What would Carol hate him for most, he wondered, when the memory of the seriousness of his crime woke him in the early hours – that he'd run the dog over in the first place, or that he'd lied to Carol when she'd insisted on him getting out of the car and checking to see what the bump had been?

He could have come clean then, but instead he'd spun her some cock and bull story about there being a kid's football in the way. Instead, he'd wrapped Meryl's body in an old blanket and stowed her away in the boot of the van. While they sat and ate their meal, each mouthful turned to dust in his mouth. Later that night, long after he'd left Carol sleeping, he'd driven to the yard where he'd dug a hole, and buried her.

When Finn was a little boy and things had gone wrong, he'd often taken refuge at his Aunty Vi's. He didn't seriously think she'd be able to help him out of the mess he was in now, but he couldn't face another day trailing round Hollyoaks with a distraught Carol, looking for Meryl, and knowing all along that she was dead.

'Rory! Lovely to see you after all this time. You must have heard me put the kettle on.'

Aunty Vi – small and bent double with age, but with a head of jet-black hair that a woman half her age would have been proud of – led Finn into the parlour and directed him to a tea chest. 'You'll have to sit there for now till I clear a space,' she said.

Finn noticed that every surface in the room was covered with Aunty Vi's clothes and clutter and wondered what was going on.

'You'll have to excuse the mess, sweetheart,' she said, 'but they're coming to collect my stuff on Monday. You must have heard I'm emigrating in a couple of weeks. Come to say your goodbyes, I guess.'

Finn perched uncomfortably on top of the tea chest. He hadn't heard, though he wasn't at all surprised, as Aunty Vi had often spoken of how she'd like to retire to Australia to be with her grandchildren.

'So you've finally decided, then?' he asked her.

He accepted the mug of tea Aunty Vi held out.

Aunty Vi said: 'I only hope I'm doing the right thing, though, Rory. I still wake up at night worrying.'

It came almost as a relief for Finn to have somebody else's problems to think about rather than his own.

'I think it's exactly the right thing, Aunty Vi. You've got no ties here after all, have you?' Finn said.

'Ah, but that's just where you're wrong, Rory. I've got my businesses for a start.'

Aunty Vi's businesses included house-sitting – which she said was much easier than babysitting as there were no nappies involved and you got to have a good poke about other people's property – and a spot of what she called 'psychic counselling'.

Finn had never been quite sure what psychic coun-selling actually involved, but had been reliably informed by Aunty Vi that she had people queuing up for her advice. Or rather the advice proffered by members of the spirit world, notably Knut, a Viking who had lived in the tenth century ~ and perished at the hands of a Norman soldier ~ and the Lady Ylaine, who'd been one of Guinevere's handmaidens and who'd met an equally nasty end in childbirth.

'Then there's Chips.'

Finn looked at his aunty in puzzlement. 'Well they have chips in Australia, Aunty Vi. They might call them by some other name but I'm sure they're just the same as British ones,' he said.

Aunty Vi smiled indulgently at Finn. 'No, silly,' she said. 'This is Chips.'

At the mention of his name, Chips bounded in. Fortunately for Finn he'd already emptied his mug down his throat. Otherwise, on his first sighting of the fluffy white poodle who'd been his aunty's constant companion for the last eight years, but who up until now had never really registered with Finn on any of his visits, he might well have spilled it all over his aunty's crimson carpet.

'If I thought Chips was going to a good home then I'd sail across the Atlantic a contented woman,' Aunty Vi said.

Finn didn't correct her mistake. What was geography when the opportunity to make up for his wrongdoing and to put an end to Carol's misery was in this very room, wagging its white, poodly tail at him?

'I'll look after him, Aunty,' he said. 'No probs, as they say down under.'

'Rory!' Aunty Vi beamed with gratitude. 'I always said you were a good boy.'

'And if there's anything else I can take off your hands while I'm here...'

'Well, I've got this hair dye. They were doing three for one at Boots, so I thought I'd stock up. Only I've decided that if I'm going to start a new life in a new country I might as well start it with a new colour. How do you think I'd look as a redhead, Rory?'

'Wonderful, Aunty Vi,' Finn replied, privately calculating just how many applications of Aunty's hair dye would be needed to transform a poodle the size of Chips into a poodle the colour of Meryl.

CHAPTER THIRTY

MADAME VIOLETTA

'It's all right, Meryl,' Carol said. 'I'll soon have you out of there.'

Meryl had done nothing but whimper all the way in the car. Carol was feeling really stressed as a result of having to drive, follow a map and pacify the dog at the same time. She decided that her appointment with Madame Violetta, Psychic Counsellor, had arrived not a moment too soon.

Her elation at getting Meryl back had soon been replaced by a feeling that something had happened to her during her absence – perhaps something so traumatic that it had caused Meryl to undergo a complete personality change. It was this change that she hoped – with the help of Madame Violetta – might be explained and hopefully reversed.

Darwin Drive was a wide tree-lined road with large, elegant detached houses either side. By contrast, Madame Violetta was small and – so Carol privately thought – looked more like the cleaning lady than the lady of the house. Her bright red hair was arranged in an ornate bun on the top of her head and the gold bangles which adorned her little fat arms chinked noisily as she led Carol into her study.

Meryl, who had started to bark excitedly as soon as Madame Violetta opened the door, struggled out of her arms and jumped up at her, wagging her tail at an alarming rate. Carol thought it odd that Meryl seemed so overjoyed to see this complete stranger.

From the way Madame Violetta picked Meryl up and hugged her, the feeling was obviously mutual. Meryl licked Madame Violetta's face enthusiastically, as if she'd been reconciled with a long-lost friend. Carol just didn't get it.

'She used to be like that with me,' she said. 'She was my best friend once.' A tear slid down her cheek and before she could help herself she was sobbing uncontrollably.

'There, there.' Madame Violetta held out a tissue which Carol accepted gratefully. 'Now sit down and tell me all about it.'

Meryl had taken refuge as far away from Carol as possible, somewhere behind Madame Violetta's feet. All Carol could hear was a contented shuffling and the occasional canine sigh of satisfaction.

'Is there anything you can do to help Meryl, Madame Violetta?' she demanded when she'd finished explaining how Meryl had gone missing and been found again. 'Only I'm at my wits' end. It's like she's a completely different dog from the one I lost.'

Madame Violetta was suddenly gripped by some kind of coughing fit. She drained a glass of water to its dregs. Carol prayed her cough wasn't catching. She couldn't possibly have any more time off work. She'd taken most of last week off trying to retrain Meryl. The poor creature had obviously been so traumatized by whatever she'd gone through that she was still barely able to remember her name. She blew her nose noisily.

'You know,' she said, 'sometimes I thinks Meryl hates me.'

By way of response, the dog growled from the depths of its hiding place.

Madame Violetta steepled her hands and furrowed her brow. 'Have you ever thought, Carol,' she said at last, 'that – er – Meryl might be punishing you for not finding her sooner?'

Carol widened her eyes as the full force of Madame Violetta's words sank in.

'You don't think she thinks I abandoned her deliberately, do you?' she said, aghast at the mere suggestion.

'Exactly that,' Madame Violetta said. She leaned forward in her chair. 'Tell me,' she said, 'who actually found Meryl in the end?'

Carol's jaw dropped open. If Madame Violetta was right, then Meryl's new found devotion to Finn – which had quickly come to replace the loathing she used to have for him – was perfectly understandable. Poor Meryl must be thinking Carol had abandoned her and Finn had rescued her, so she'd responded with doggy logic, simply transferring her affections from Carol to Finn.

'I see it all now,' she said.

Madame Violetta had closed her eyes and was starting to sway from side to side in her seat. 'No, Carol,' she said, 'I'm afraid there's more. I'm getting something.'

Carol pulled herself upright in her seat. She was beginning to wonder when the 'psychic' bit would come in. Things were starting to get exciting. Madame Violetta placed both palms down on the table in front of her.

'Knut is coming through, Carol. He has a message for you.'

Carol swallowed hard. She didn't think she knew any Knuts. Although there had been a lad called Stefan in Southport once.

'Knut knows Meryl from another life. She was a Viking dog once. Water is her medium.'

'Really?' Carol thought of Meryl with a new-found respect.

'Knut says that Meryl is grieving because you took her away from the water. What water did you take her away from, Carol?'

Carol racked her brains. 'The only water I can think of is the water that was leaking into Finn's boat.'

Madame Violetta caught her breath, then began to nod her head again and again excitedly. 'That's it, Carol,' she said. 'Knut says you removed Meryl from her element. She needed to work something out from another life and the only way she could do it was to remain on that boat until she had.'

'But the boat went down,' Carol explained.

'As far as Meryl was concerned you took the boat away from her. You denied her the opportunity to work out this...other thing. As a punishment, she ran away from you. Unfortunately, Carol, somehow the cycle has been broken.'

Madame Violetta blinked awake.

Carol was aghast. 'You mean, she'll always hate me? Is there nothing we can do?'

'Oh, yes, sweetheart,' Madame Violetta said, training her beady eyes on Carol. 'Five more sessions should do it. Fifteen quid a time.'

CHAPTER THIRTY-ONE

RAISING THE BOAT

Finn had been obsessed with raising the boat for some time. He knew how to do it – he'd spent ages reading up about it – but he couldn't do it on his own. He would need a lot of help. Each morning he strolled down to the spot where he knew she'd gone down and stared wistfully into the water.

He needed a place of his own – desperately. He hated sharing with Lewis and Ruth. He didn't know which was worse, Lewis pretending he was welcome to stay as long as he liked or Ruth not pretending at all.

Tony wasn't happy about him staying with Carol rent-free either, and Finn suspected that any day now he would raise the subject of him chipping in to pay the bills. Finn was a generous guy by nature, but the thought of any money of his finding its way into Tony's pocket always stuck in his craw.

In all the time Tony had been cooking at Deva, Finn had never once given him a tip – apart from once telling him that if he used English mustard in his barbecue sauce instead of French, his Creole sausages would have a bit more bite to them.

Then there was Meryl. Or rather Chips. He couldn't look at Carol or the poodle without feeling guilty, but he knew he was in too deep ever to get out now. Fortunately, Carol and Chips/Meryl seemed to be hitting it off better than before, and at first Finn had been grateful to Madame Violetta for helping the two of them sort out their differences.

When the penny had dropped and Finn realized it was his own dear Aunty Vi who was practising her psychic counselling on Carol and Meryl, he'd expected to be rumbled – and soon. But so far, so good. As luck would have it, Carol and Meryl's last session had taken place the previous day. According to Carol, this coincided with Madame Violetta leaving for Australia to live with her grandchildren at the end of the week. Finn could breathe easily again and devote all his energy into organizing the raising of the barge.

Students, in his experience, would do anything for a few free pints. Pretty soon he had enough volunteers to raise the *Titanic*, let alone his little houseboat. When word got round that Finn was going to finance a party with as much free food and booze as his helpers could consume, he had students stopping him in the street volunteering their services.

When his mission had been accomplished and a rather bedraggled barge was finally dredged out of the water and safely winched into the air and on to dry land, Finn decided it was time to come clean about exactly how he was going to finance the party. So far there'd been no sign of food or alcohol and Lewis and Carol weren't the only ones to start asking questions about when the party was going to start. A bit of wheeling and dealing was called for – but then again, those were Finn's middle names.

'Oh, ye of little faith,' Finn said to his weary gang of volunteers, who were all beginning to think they'd been conned.

Finn disappeared for a moment but was soon back with several buckets which he distributed to the bemused students.

'What's this?' Lewis said, reading the label on the bucket he'd been handed. 'It says, "The Cleopatra project for underprivileged students. Please give generously."'

'And now the *pièce de résistance*. Come along, Carol. I want you at the prow. My Cleopatra.'

A blushing Carol allowed herself to be led by the hand on to the boat, accompanied by the cheers of helpers who had decided to enter into the spirit of things. Finn had known all along that his plan would work but he had to admit to holding his breath as he threw a magnificent cloak around Carol's shoulders. If she refused to join in, then his whole plan was doomed to failure.

Fortunately, Carol, blushing to the roots of her hair, seemed genuinely pleased at being singled out like that.

'Oh, Finn,' she said, kissing him on the nose, 'you're a twit. But I do love you.'

The people of Chester gave generously to the Cleopatra Project. Soon all the buckets were full and the barge, Carol clutching Meryl at the prow, arrived safely in Finn's yard.

It was as Carol and Meryl were bumped unceremoni-ously on to the ground that Meryl gave a yelp and momentarily slipped from Carol's grasp.

'Oh no, you don't!' Carol yelled as she retrieved Meryl from the watery depths of the barge. 'Oh God, look at you. You're all oily. Chuck us a rag, somebody.'

She began to clean Meryl up, hoping none of the oil the dog seemed to have picked up on her brief escape would come off on her Cleopatra cloak. She fancied wearing this at the party. And maybe later on, even – when everyone had gone and she and Finn were on their own. Her imagination about what that might lead to in the night ahead began to take flight and she subjected Meryl to an even more enthusiastic bout of rag-rubbing. The poodle protested with a series of yelps. Carol apologized to Meryl for her vigour and removed the cloth – now black and smelling a bit peculiar – from around her anxious little body.

Finn heard the scream from where he was on the other side of the yard, helping Tony to set up his barbecue, and froze. His instinct told him right away that Carol had discovered Meryl's true identity. He'd been rumbled.

CHAPTER THIRTY-TWO

HAIR TODAY

Finn hadn't got so mullered in a long time. After the party, he must have fallen asleep long after everyone else had left, sprawled out on the floor of the shed, fully clothed. His head throbbed and his mouth felt like the bottom of a hamster's cage. His first thought was coffee and lots of it. His second thought was Carol.

He groaned when he remembered the events of the previous day and sank his head in his hands. How could he ever face her again? Carol's fury had known no bounds when she'd discovered her poodle was suddenly a different colour from the one she remembered.

Her shrieks had brought not only Finn running but practically everyone else too. Carol's hands were covered in black dye and Meryl/Chips was cowering on her lap, wondering what all the fuss was about.

It had taken both Lewis and Tony to pull Carol – half Finn's size – off him, when he finally admitted what he'd done. They should have left her to kill him quickly, Finn was thinking, as he sloped into Deva. Justice would have been done, for one thing. For another, you can only die once. Nervously, he checked behind him. He was fully expecting another attack at any moment. This time, he would meet his fate like a man.

The moment he walked into Deva, all heads swivelled in his direction. Finn wished the earth would open up and swallow him. It was just like a scene from one of those old John Wayne movies, he thought. The stranger walks into the bar, the pianist stops playing and all conversation immediately ceases.

'Make mine a bourbon,' he said to Mr Morgan, who was looking at Finn as if he had two heads.

'No alcohol without food at this hour,' Mr Morgan said. 'You know the law.'

'Sorry,' Finn mumbled. 'I was miles away. I meant a coffee.'

'Bit of a hairy night, eh?' Mr Morgan said. He was sniggering so much he spilled coffee in the saucer and had to get Finn another one.

Finn paid up and shuffled over to an empty table. Complete strangers were staring at him. He wondered if everyone in Hollyoaks had heard about the terrible thing he'd done to Carol. Tony approached him cautiously.

'Bacon butty,' he said. 'On the house.'

He stared at Finn and held out the plate.

Finn had had enough. 'Look, mate,' he said. 'What is it with everyone in here this morning? Has my hair turned green or something?'

Tony sat down next to him and Finn began to tuck into his free brunch.

'Er – funny you should say that, Finn.'

Finn stopped chewing and frowned.

'You, er, seen a mirror this morning?'

'I don't need to see a mirror. I know what I look like. According to Carol I've got horns and a pitchfork and 666 tattooed on my scalp,' Finn said. 'If that's an accurate description of the spawn of Satan – 'cos that's how she described me yesterday.'

A colourful selection of Carol's other phrases from last night popped into his head. By comparison 'spawn of Satan' was quite affectionate.

Tony was grinning at him.

'I don't see what's so funny, mate,' Finn said. 'Carol will never speak to me again.'

'How many times have I heard that before?' Tony said. 'Only this time you're spot on. When I last spoke to her she was packing.'

Finn felt like all the blood had just drained from his body. Packing? Leaving? Without giving him a chance to explain? He had to speak to her before she left.

'She won't see you, Finn. You'd be wasting your time even trying to talk to her, honestly.'

Finn stared at his half-eaten bacon butty. He couldn't eat another mouthful.

'You should really look in a mirror, you know, Finn,' Tony said. 'I'm telling you for your own good.'

'I don't need a mirror,' Finn insisted. 'I can find my own throat without looking at it. Just pass me a razor.'

Lewis breezed in. When he saw Finn he stopped dead at his table and burst out laughing.

'What on earth have you done to your hair?' he demanded.

Tentatively, Finn put his hand up to his head.

'I did tell you,' Tony said. 'You can't say you weren't warned.'

'Pass us a spoon, would you, Tony,' Finn said.

Tony obliged. Finn brought the spoon up close to his face and peered into it.

'Ah,' he said, at last. 'Not green. Pink. She's done a very good job, all things considered.' He turned his head round as far as it would go for Tony and Lewis to get a better look. 'What's it like at the back?' he asked.

CHAPTER THIRTY-THREE

GONE TOMORROW

'Which bit of "bugger off" don't you understand, Finn?'

Carol had eventually let Finn into the flat, but so far she'd managed to avoid looking at him, busy as she was chucking things into a suitcase. Every now and then she ticked something off on a list she'd drawn up earlier. Finn had never seen her so organized.

'Please, Carol,' Finn said. 'Will you just sit down for five minutes. All I need is a bit of time to explain.'

Carol rolled her eyes dramatically.

'You think five minutes is long enough to talk your way out of this little lot?' she wanted to know. 'Ever seen that film *The Greatest Story Ever Told*? Well, it's got nothing on this one.'

'I know what you must think of me, Carol,' he said.

'Wrong,' Carol replied. 'How can you? It's not possible, Finn, because I don't think anything of you at all. So get lost.' With every word she uttered, she threw something else into her case.

'You're angry,' Finn went on. 'You're not thinking straight.'

That was a mistake – he knew it as soon as he'd said it. Carol pushed him into a chair with a pair of trainers.

'Right!' she shouted, her face contorted with anger.

'That's enough. How dare you say I'm not thinking straight after everything you've done?'

Finn could do nothing but wait for Carol to get into her stride. She paced up and down, reminding Finn of every stupid thing he'd done in all the time she'd known him. It was quite a long list.

'This latest stunt is the best yet,' she shouted, when she'd finally got to the end of it. She threw a pair of jeans into her case, followed by a sweatshirt. 'Not only do you run my dog over, but you think that if you get another one and dye it black I won't notice the difference.'

Finn blinked. 'You didn't, Carol,' he said.

'Oh, I didn't, did I?' she demanded. 'Well, if that's the case, can you explain to me why I forked out ninety quid to have Meryl – or whatever she's called – psycho-analysed?' She retrieved the sweatshirt from the case, checked the label and threw it at Finn. 'I believe that's yours,' she added.

Finn was about to say thank you, but Carol resumed her attack on him before he could get the word out.

'I knew that dog wasn't Meryl as soon as she wagged her tail when you walked in,' she said. 'Meryl hated you. She had better instincts than I ever did when it came to men. I should have listened to her right at the start as far as you were concerned!'

Finn hung his head in shame. It was beginning to look like he was fighting a losing battle.

'I only did what I did with the dye because I was afraid to own up to, you know...'

'You can say it,' Carol said. 'It's a bit late to start getting coy about murder.'

'I didn't run over her deliberately, Carol. It was an accident,' Finn said. 'But then one thing led to another and the more I tried to get out of it the more difficult it was. You have every right to call me a coward.'

'I don't need your permission to call you a coward, Finn,' Carol said. 'Or a liar or a cheat or a bastard or a complete bullshitter. Now will you please leave. I've got things to do.'

Shamefaced, Finn got up. There was absolutely nothing he could say or do to remedy the situation, but he gave it one last shot.

'I love you, Carol,' he said. 'I swear I'd kill myself before I hurt you deliberately.'

'There's a sharp knife in the kitchen drawer. Want me to get it for you?'

Finn couldn't be sure, but Carol looked as if she was blinking back a tear. Just a few more words, and maybe he could get her to change her mind.

'You're the only girl I've ever loved, Carol. Honest.'

Carol smiled bitterly. 'Well, if that's the way you show it, Finn, then I don't want your love,' she said, with a finality that cut Finn to the quick. 'I'm going away to get my head together first thing tomorrow. Now, you know where the door is. Go through it. It's your choice whether you open it first or not.'

Finn wanted to protest, but he knew for certain now that it was too late. He'd never seen Carol so cold.

'Will you be you going in Beryl?' he asked her at the door.

She gave a curt nod.

'I'll check the oil for you before you go, if you want,' he offered.

'I don't think so, Finn,' Carol replied. 'I'll manage on my own from now on, thank you very much.'

'Right, then,' Finn mumbled as he let himself out.

CHAPTER THIRTY-FOUR

TONY'S PHILOSOPHY

Finn had decided to turn over a new leaf. He was done with his old ways. He intended throwing himself into the business and never looking at another woman again.

'I've finished with the lot of them, Tony,' he remarked one lunchtime, over a buttered barm cake at Deva. 'From now on I intend to live the celibate life.'

Tony reckoned that given Finn's history this was highly unlikely, but Finn was insistent.

'You tried getting back with Carol?' he asked Finn. 'I'm sure you only need to say the word and you'd be in like a shot.'

Finn shook his head. 'If I've learned anything from my mistakes,' he said, 'it's that you've got to know when something's dead and buried.'

'Pity you didn't consider letting Carol know that Meryl was dead as soon as you ran over her,' Tony said, grinning at his own wit. 'That way none of this would have happened.'

'Thank you, Tony,' Finn said. 'That'll do. Another of your finest buttered barm cakes, if you please. If I want wisecracks on the side I'll ask for them.'

'Seen much of Carol since she got back?'

'Oh, you know – we've exchanged a few words.'

Finn was hedging around the question, but he didn't want Tony to see how cut up about Carol he still was. Her most recent brush-off was surely the cruellest one of all and one he still couldn't believe had happened.

It had been just the day before that Carol, back from her little holiday, had strolled back into the yard as cool as a cucumber to say that she'd forgiven Finn for what he'd done to Meryl.

'It was just a bit of bad judgement on your part,' she'd said. 'I had a lot of time to think when I was away and I realized that you never really meant to do what you did. Can we be friends again, Finn?'

Finn had been over the moon, already making mental plans for a night of passion on the boat with Carol – the first of many more, he hoped. But Carol must have seen the gleam in his eye, because her next words quickly dashed his hopes.

'Friends, Finn,' she said. 'Not lovers, remember.'

And then she'd walked off. Just like that. It was almost harder to cope with than her hating him. After everything they'd been through together he had been relegated to a casual acquaintance. The whole exchange – building up his hopes and then dashing them – had been like a vicious slap in the face. He couldn't allow himself to be put through that again, for his own sanity.

'All relationships are doomed from the off anyway these days, if you ask me,' Tony said. 'I should know.'

Finn knew that Tony had been down recently because his parents had split up. In fact, he'd even made a few stupid jokes about it.

'Still no signs of them getting back together?' he asked.

Tony shook his head. 'They're further away than ever,' he said. 'But I'm determined to get them back together.'

'Well, good luck to you,' Finn said. 'I'm off to the yard to sort out that load from this morning's house clearance,' he said, draining his coffee cup. 'Maybe I'll see you later in the Dog.'

CHAPTER THIRTY-FIVE

VICTORIA

It was a slow morning. Finn had already laughed at his horoscope and done the crossword. He was rooting through a pile of stuff he'd picked up at his last house clearance, wondering if any of it might make him any money at the next yard sale, when someone came into the yard.

It was a woman. Now, Finn had sworn an oath that after Carol he wasn't even going to look at another woman in lust, but this was different.

He watched her as she rummaged through a box of trinkets, smiling quietly whenever she saw something she liked the look of and occasionally holding it up to the light. By the looks of things, Finn thought, this was a prospective customer, and he hadn't seen many of those all week.

'Is there anything I can help you with?' he asked in his best salesman's voice.

She looked up at him and smiled. Finn felt a stirring in his loins he'd not felt for some time.

'Well, actually there might be,' she said. 'I'm looking for a housewarming present for a friend of mine. Nothing too pricey but with a bit of, you know – style.'

'Style,' Finn repeated, allowing his eyes to travel over

her face and down her body while she continued to browse. Style was something this woman had in abundance, he decided.

'If you'll just wait there,' he said and brought out a lamp that he'd been admiring only half an hour before she came in. 'Would this be the sort of thing you're looking for?'

She caught her breath in delight as she took the lamp from him. Her long nails were painted red, he noticed. He had a sudden erotic vision of them running along the length of his back and quickly looked away. He should be ashamed of himself. She was old enough to be someone's mother.

'This is simply exquisite,' she breathed, then her face fell. 'Only really I was looking for a pair.'

'A pair?' Finn's eyes were level with her chest. When he looked up she was looking back, completely unfazed. Finn was beginning to sense that whatever he was feeling, she was feeling it too.

'Look,' she said. 'If I left you my telephone number, would it be convenient for you to ring me should you run across a partner for this one?'

Finn looked on while she wrote down her details. She was slim, blonde, well dressed. Maybe she did have a few miles on her clock, but from what he could see her engine was still ticking over nicely. And as for the bodywork…

'Here's my number, er…'

Finn quickly introduced himself.

'And I'm Victoria,' she replied. 'You can call me Vicky.'

And you can call me any time, Finn thought, as he followed her slow, sexy exit out of the yard.

'I have seen the future,' he said dreamily to an empty yard. 'And it's called Victoria.'

CHAPTER THIRTY-SIX

A DISCOVERY

Victoria. Vicky. Vick. No, not Vick. Wasn't that something you rubbed on your chest when you had a cold? Finn took in his appearance in the mirror at the Dog and was impressed. He'd spent most of the afternoon sprucing himself up. He'd even nipped into Debenham's in town for a squirt of that YSL Live Jazz malarkey. He was keen to get everything just right.

Never before had he taken so much trouble with his appearance. Somehow he suspected that little things – like not having holes in your socks or making sure you had clean fingernails – would be really important to Victoria. For a start, she had a longer past than most girls he'd been out with and he didn't want to be compared too unfavourably with any of the men who figured in it.

'Don't rush it, man,' he warned himself. So far, so good. He'd found her a matching lamp, followed it up with a phone call and she'd been delighted. One thing was slowly leading to another and he had a feeling that this next visit was the visit in which they'd finally get naked. Or was he jumping the gun slightly?

He'd been there an hour at least and Vicky still hadn't mentioned anything about the bits and pieces she wanted valuing, which was the reason Finn thought he'd been invited in the first place – though all along he'd been living in hope that her invitation was really for something much more intimate.

'I don't believe you could be so naive, Finn,' Vicky said when he raised the subject of valuation. She was serving him a second helping of something she called 'poulet andalousienne'.

'It was a ploy, that was all,' she laughed, 'so that I could get you here and have my wicked way with you.'

She was flushed from the wine and her blonde hair, which had been neatly and firmly restrained in an elegant bun when Finn first arrived, was now escaping in soft tendrils down her slender neck.

Finn played for time. With any other female giving him the green light like that, he'd have launched himself at her with no further thought. But he'd never met a woman as sophisticated as Victoria before. He needed to be one hundred per cent certain that he'd been reading the signals right. Not to mention the fact that he was, he had to admit, slightly intimidated. But in a good way.

'You're a hard woman, Victoria,' Finn said, trying to keep his cool. He pushed his plate to one side. In his experience, sex and food didn't mix, whatever they tried to tell you in the movies.

'What about you, Finn?' Vicky was out of her chair now and on his lap. 'Are you a hard man?'

There was no doubt at all what Victoria was getting at and the softness of her breasts beneath her silk shirt, combined with the taste of her lips soon had the desired effect on Finn.

'We could go upstairs,' Victoria whispered.

'If you think I'd get a better feel for your bits and pieces up there, then perhaps we should,' Finn said.

She smelt of perfume and cooking and was driving

him wild. Together, they lurched out of the dining room – clutching the wine and each other – and stumbled up the stairs into her bedroom, where they both collapsed on to the bed.

Any nerves that Finn may have been suffering at the prospect of having to perform in the bed – where once Victoria had lain with her now estranged husband – soon vanished in the heat of the moment.

Afterwards, they lay in each other's arms in blissful exhaustion.

'Not bad for a callow youth,' Victoria teased him.

Finn was flattered. He thought he'd died and gone to heaven and couldn't wait for a second helping. First things first, however. He put out a hand and groped for the bottle of wine.

'Empty,' he said.

'There's another in the fridge. Be a lamb and nip downstairs for it,' Vicky said.

Finn slid out of bed – a touch shyly, considering that five minutes before Vicky had been exploring parts of his body that not even the doctor had seen in close-up – and crept out of the room.

They say pride comes before a fall. Finn was feeling ridiculously proud of his sexual prowess as he lingered for a moment on the landing to get his bearings. He picked up a framed photo of a man and a boy playing snooker. He was curious to find out a bit more about her and the family she spoke about occasionally.

So this was the son – the young man who took after his father in everything including name. The businessman who, in his mother's words, was destined to become a millionaire before he reached the age of thirty. Finn stared closer at the photo and did a double take, his eyes suddenly going wide with horror. The smug face that looked out at Finn from the photograph was that of his mate, Tony Hutchinson.

A sultry voice from the bedroom knocked him out of his near-catatonic state.

'Have you got the wine yet, Tiger? I'm not sure I can wait much longer for a refill.'

He'd just shagged Tony's mum. How the bloody hell was he going to get out of this one?

CHAPTER THIRTY-SEVEN

DISCOVERY

Everywhere he looked, Tony was there. In Deva, chatting to customers; in the Dog, drinking his lager; in the yard, getting a bit of sun. He was like a vengeful ghost, Finn thought, stalking him to make him pay for his crime. Any minute now he expected him to point an accusing finger at him and tell him exactly how much he knew about Finn and his mother. Quite frankly, it was doing Finn's head in.

When he told Lewis exactly who the mysterious older woman he'd been seeing for the past few weeks was, Lewis thought it was hilarious.

'You're going to have to finish it, though, Finn,' he added. 'I mean – somebody's mum. It's a bit off limits.'

Finn had visions of Vicky taking Tony to nursery school, Vicky feeding Tony baby food in his high chair, Vicky changing Tony's nappy. Off limits? It was absolutely disgusting.

'Thing is, Lewis,' he said, 'I fancy her like mad. I can't give her up.'

'Well, you'd better get used to the idea of Tony knocking your block off when he finds out, then,' Lewis said.

Later, Vicky came to the barge to see Finn, and to talk about how he felt now that he'd discovered who she was.

'I can understand if you want to end it, Finn,' she said. 'But why should it matter that I'm Tony's mother?'

When she kissed him, Finn briefly forgot why.

'I'm still a woman, first and foremost, remember,' she said. 'Tony's an important part of my life but so are you now. Why should we have to choose? Now come here and kiss me.'

Finn obliged, but he still didn't feel right about it.

'I think you'd better leave before Tony sees you hanging around,' he said nervously.

Victoria laughed teasingly. 'Oh come on, Finn,' she said. 'You're not frightened of Tony, surely. And here was I thinking you were such a big strong boy.'

Nervously, Finn peeked through the window. There was Tony again, staring at the boat. He thought his heart was going to give up.

There was a knock and then Tony called out, 'Only me! Brought you both some coffee on the house.'

Finn motioned to Vicky to hide and opened up the awning just enough to see Tony's curious face.

'Is she here?' he hissed. 'Your fancy woman? Only everyone's saying you've got her locked away inside your boat. When are you going to introduce us?'

'Not now, Tony,' Finn said, quaking in his boots. 'Thanks for the coffees, though.'

Tony retreated, disappointed. It wasn't fair, he thought, that everyone had got a glimpse of Finn's older woman, apart from him. Carol had seen her, although she'd been a bit vague when Tony had asked for a description. Lewis had even been invited into the barge to meet her.

Well, he swore he'd find out who she was if it was the last thing he did. He decided he'd wait outside in the dark until they came out. From the sounds of things there soon wouldn't be any oxygen left inside that boat. They'd have to come out soon to get some air.

It was dark when Tony heard the muffled footsteps of Finn and his new woman as they emerged from their hiding place, giggling and shushing each other as they did so. As the two of them emerged, Tony flashed his torch at them.

At first he thought there'd been some mistake. She'd come to look for him and got lost and then been to Finn's to ask for directions – that was it. But then he caught the look on their faces. It was a horrible mixture of satisfied lust and guilt.

'Mum!' was all Tony could say. 'What's going on?'

CHAPTER THIRTY-EIGHT

PEACE OFFERING

'I can't give you up, Vicky. I was mad to think I could.'

Finn and Vicky were lying in bed, taking refuge from an irate Tony. Finn was beginning to understand how it must feel to have a contract out on your life. Every shadow was Tony's and with each tap on the shoulder, his blood ran cold.

'Don't you think you're being a bit over-dramatic, Finn?' Vicky asked him when he expressed these thoughts to her. 'I mean, what can Tony actually do to you?'

That afternoon, in the Dog, when Tony had turned on him, completely livid, Finn had made a firm resolution not to stick around to find out.

'You worry too much about Tony's feelings,' Vicky said. 'It's none of his business whom I share my bed with. We're both consenting adults, after all.'

Finn had thought long and hard about his relationship with both Vicky and Tony. He felt sick with guilt because Tony had fallen out with his mum big time due to her relationship with Finn. Family feuds were horrible things, as he knew from his own experience. The last thing he wanted was to be the cause of Tony and Vicky never speaking again.

But, at the same time, he really liked Vicky and she really liked him. And as she was quick to insist, Tony was no longer a child who needed to be sheltered from the stickier facts of life, after all. He should get his own life and let Vicky get on with hers.

'You're right.' Finn nuzzled Vicky's ear. 'We can't let Tony dictate the terms of our relationship. I was a pillock to even think of giving you up just to spare his feelings.'

Vicky rolled on to her side and sat up.

'Finn,' she said in a voice that warned him she was about to ask a great favour.

'Mmm?' He was admiring the view of her naked body and wondering if there was time to repeat their last performance before he met Lewis.

Earlier, in Deva, he'd overheard some students saying that the college hall had been double-booked for the end-of-year ball and unless someone came up with another venue pretty quickly, the ball wouldn't take place. Immediately it had occurred to Finn that the yard would be an ideal place to hold a summer ball. He could picture it now – St Tropez in Chester. After all, he would be only too willing to provide a yacht. And what did it take to knock together a few palm trees?

'This business venture you just told me about, would there be any room for Tony in it?'

'I don't think we need a comedian,' he joked. 'I thought a DJ would be a better idea.'

She gave him a playful push. 'I'm talking about the food, you idiot,' she said. 'You see, that's part of your problem with Tony. You never let up on him for a minute. He's my son, you know. And I love him in spite of everything.'

Finn hung his head sheepishly and promised to leave Tony alone. 'It'll be difficult, though,' he said. 'It's got to be a bit of a habit with me over the years.'

'So what do you think?'

'I think you're gorgeous.'

'About Tony doing the food, idiot.'

Finn frowned. 'You mean I'd have to hand money over to him?'

Vicky gave an exasperated sigh. 'Think about it,' she said. 'Tony couldn't refuse.'

'Well, I've never known him turn down an offer of money yet,' Finn admitted.

'True,' Vicky agreed. 'He's always been a chip off the old block. But think how mature it would make you look, Finn, if you were the first to offer the hand of friendship. He wouldn't dare refuse for fear of looking petty.'

Privately, Finn couldn't help thinking that looking petty had never bothered Tony before, but he kept quiet. Lying here in the buff being snide about his girlfriend's son put him in a very vulnerable position.

'I'd thought about asking Mr Morgan,' Finn said.

Vicky moved closer and started to do something very seductive with her tongue and his ear. 'Do it for me,' she whispered. 'P–lease.'

'I could be persuaded, I suppose,' he groaned.

'Does this persuade you, Finn? Or this?'

'I'll have to get the contract first,' Finn said, before abandoning himself to Vicky's reviving touch. 'Aaaah!'

'Please, Finn.'

'Oh, go on, then.'

CHAPTER THIRTY-NINE

D-I-V-O-R-C-E

Finn got the contract and Tony agreed to do the food. Finn should have known from the way he agreed so readily that it meant trouble. When Tony told him he wanted one thousand pounds with five hundred up front to provide top quality seafood to go with the St Tropez theme, Finn kept a firm grip, reminding himself that he was doing this for Victoria.

'I hope when I have children, Tony, that they don't turn out to be as mean and grasping as you are,' he said.

Tony's face turned grey. Finn suspected Tony would be on to his father immediately to warn him that his firstborn son's inheritance was in danger of being snatched from under his nose by rival claimants – the as-yet-unborn children of his ex-wife and her new lover.

It gave him some small satisfaction for the rest of the day that he'd managed to put the wind up Tony. Winding Tony up about himself and Vicky was becoming a more and more addictive leisure pursuit as each day passed. It wasn't long before he decided he needed another fix.

Tony was on the phone when he opened the door to Deva. Finn stopped dead when he heard his name.

'Finn. That's it. Tall, rough looking, lives on a boat.'

Finn's stomach gave a lurch. So, his suspicions were correct, then. Tony was going to have him taken out by a ruthless contract killer. His days were numbered. Would it be a bullet in the back in a busy shopping street at high noon, or did his killer prefer to carry out this grisly task in the dead of night? Slowly…painfully. He gulped.

Tony's next words, though, didn't tally with the gruesome scenario Finn was playing and replaying in his head.

'I'm sorry you and Mum are getting a divorce, Dad. But if anyone's to blame, that Finn is. I don't blame you for citing him in the least. He deserves to be dragged through every court in the land.'

'Thanks for the vote of confidence,' Finn muttered. 'Nice to know you're as keen on me as I am on you.'

He missed the rest of the conversation because he was so worried about the snippet he'd heard. So Vicky and Tony's dad were really going through with the divorce, then? Well, he was glad even if Tony wasn't. He heard Tony put the phone down, then suddenly there he was.

'You!'

'Is that how you greet all your customers?' Finn asked him. 'What happened to "Would you like to see the menu?"'

Tony snarled at him: 'Marriage breaker. I suppose you're happy now?'

'Listen, mate,' Finn said, 'I've tried to be reasonable about this. But when are you going to get it? I had nothing to do with your parents splitting up. Their marriage has been over for years.'

Tony lurched towards Finn, a murderous look in his eyes. 'Get out!' he yelled. 'Just get out of here and don't show your face again.'

Arguing with Tony was a waste of breath, Finn decided. He had no intention of staying around here to be insulted. He had a lot to do. The college ball might be a lucrative deal for him, but there was a lot of work to be done on the yard and on the boat before either was in any fit state to host it.

'Don't worry, I'm off,' he said. 'Might just pop over to see your mum. You know, to give her my congratulations on finally shaking off the shackles.'

He legged it before Tony could get round the counter to reach him.

Later, Victoria showed up at the yard. Finn was putting the finishing touches to a palm tree.

'I'm sorry you had to hear about the divorce through Tony, Finn,' she said. 'I wanted to tell you myself.'

Finn put down his paintbrush.

'I never thought Tony's father would cite another man as co-respondent,' she said. 'Not with his sexual history.'

'Puts it about a bit, does he?'

'You could say that.' Vicky sighed. 'I stopped caring about what he did years ago, Finn. But I care about you. Divorce can be a messy business.'

'Look, I really don't mind,' Finn said. 'I can handle it.' Vicky looked so forlorn that he went to give her a big hug. '*We* can handle it.'

'And then there's the age gap,' she sighed. 'I wouldn't blame you if you wanted to finish it, Finn. There must be easier relationships.'

Finn stopped her complaining with a kiss.

'If I'd have wanted an easy relationship,' he said, 'I'd have bought a hamster. Now, come here and give us another kiss.'

CHAPTER FORTY

TONY'S REVENGE

The ball started off well enough. The yard was ready in time – just. Finn had managed to get a DJ, the boat looked surprisingly convincing as a yacht – well, to those people who'd never seen a yacht – and Finn had worked wonders decking out the food area with tables and lanterns.

Things started to go downhill when Tony arrived with the food. Finn rubbed his hands together in anticipation of the nautical spread Tony had prepared. He had visions of lobster, crab, whole salmon on stainless steel plates and giant prawns just waiting to be gutted and dunked into a delicate seafood sauce.

It was Finn who was gutted when he saw what Tony had actually spent his money on. And had there been any seafood sauce on view, he would have drowned Tony in it there and then.

'What the...?' he gasped.

With a flourish, Tony lifted the lid off one particular platter to reveal a dish of ocean sticks. He laid out the rest of the spread, which consisted of fish-shaped chicken nuggets, fish fingers and imitation prawns. Finn looked on dumbfounded until everything had been set out, hardly believing his eyes. By that time, if Tony had brought out a couple of buckets of maggots he wouldn't have been surprised. While he worked, Finn could have sworn Tony was singing under his breath. 'Mum's gone to Iceland,' it sounded like.

'What do you call this?' Finn spluttered.

'I call this revenge, Finn,' Tony said. 'Sweetest thing I've ever tasted.'

Finn was speechless with rage. Why he didn't deck Tony there and then he didn't know. Somewhere in the darkest recesses of his brain there lurked the certain knowledge that if he did Vicky would never forgive him.

'You're not truly trying to tell me you've spent five hundred quid on this?' he said when he finally managed to find his voice from deep in the pit of his stomach where it had been hiding. 'What about the rest of my money?'

'There's labour costs to be taken into consideration, remember?' Tony said. 'Then there's my insurance. Have you any idea how much one of these crystal bowls is worth? Five hundred pounds is nothing. And remember, you still owe me the other half.'

Finn gripped the table in disbelief and fury at Tony's cheek. 'Of all the petty minded, pathetic tricks,' he said.

From then on the night was ruined as far as Finn was concerned. Tony disappeared to get off his face on the fruit punch as fast as he'd arrived, leaving Finn to deal with the complaints from students – which came thick and fast. It was no use bluffing his way out of it this time with talk of high overheads and the extortionate cost of labour. He had to promise everyone a refund.

Tony had won, and from the look of smug satisfaction on his face he was enjoying every second of his victory. Finn was consumed with hatred for the sneaky, conniving, spiteful bastard. Everything ruined, after all the work he'd put in.

Next day, he marched round to see Vicky and tell her exactly what Tony had done. He was amazed that she didn't seem to believe him.

'Look, Vicky, I'm not making this up!' he shouted. 'Your son is a rip-off merchant. I've been trying to tell you that for months and you always laugh if off. Well, you can't laugh it off any longer.'

'How dare you talk about my son like that?' Vicky shouted back. 'He's a highly qualified chef. Why would he want to rip you off?'

'Oh, think about it, Vicky,' he yelled. Women could be very dense at times, Finn thought. 'Your son has ruined my reputation!'

Vicky laughed. 'What reputation is this exactly? From what I heard your reputation has been in shreds for some time.'

Finn was exasperated. 'I'm talking about Lewis and me. The reputation we have for providing the public with value-for-money club nights,' he said. 'They'll never come to anything we organize ever again after this. And it's all your fault!'

Vicky narrowed her eyes. 'And how exactly do you work that out?'

Finn was too livid to care that her manner and her voice were suddenly frosty. He was here to say his piece and say it he would. Whatever the consequences.

'Because if you hadn't persuaded me to offer your poxy arsewipe of a son this catering contract, none of this would have happened. Now I'm five hundred quid down – plus I've got to find a fortune to refund everybody's ticket money.'

'I don't think you and I have anything more to say to each other,' Vicky said, sending the temperature plummeting from frosty to ice-cool.

Finn was shocked, but he'd gone too far to back down. 'If that's the way you want it then that's fine by me.'

He strode to the door and opened it with a flourish. 'If you see your beloved son before I do just tell him that I intend to get that money back if I have to squeeze it out of him. And I don't care which end it comes out of.'

CHAPTER FORTY-ONE

BOYCOTT!

'BOYCOTT DEVA!
THIS FOOD IS COOKED BY A FRAUD!'

Finn surveyed the sign he'd just painted.

'I'll show that snivellin' little toe-rag of a thief he can't mess with me,' Finn muttered.

Since the ball and his row with Vicky, Finn had been brooding over how he could get his own back on Tony. His whole life was collapsing in a heap around him and all because of that miserable scrote.

Well, he thought, as he paraded up and down outside Deva, holding up his sign to anyone who happened to be contemplating popping in for a quick bite to eat, Tony was about to get his. With knobs on.

He'd already had a visit from some snooper who said he was a reporter from the college magazine wanting to know what had really gone on at the college ball.

'I am completely blameless in all this,' he'd told the guy, before spending ten minutes verbally putting the boot into Tony. The reporter had nodded in all the right places but it was a well-known fact that papers were full of lies. Finn should know, he'd never read one in his life.

He'd had a word with Lewis to get him to speak to Ruth – a former editor of the paper – about putting their side of the story, but Ruth had said point blank that she no longer had any influence on what was reported, so there was no point even asking her to speak to the present editor. When she'd seen how distraught the two of them were, however, she'd relented and promised to do what she could and put a good word in. But Finn wasn't holding his breath.

For most of the morning he stood there, drawing curious glances from customers who for the most part pretended he was invisible. Finn was starting to suspect he wasn't really having much success getting his message across, and put it down to the fact that kids nowadays had never been taught the first rule of student politics: never cross a picket line. Second only to don't put your hand in your pocket at the bar unless it's for a game of pocket billiards.

He was so deep in thought that he didn't notice Tony staring out at him through Deva's window. Finn gave him the finger and waggled the sign at him. Unfortunately, Mr Morgan saw the whole thing. He was quick, but not quick enough to prevent Tony from rushing outside and attempting to wrestle Finn to the ground. The two of them started in on each other like a couple of WWF veterans.

'Why don't you stop hounding my family and leave my mother to get on with her life!' Tony yelled.

Finn managed to slip from Tony's grasp and land a punch on him.

'Aargh! Take that, mother-snatcher!' cried Tony, taking a swing back.

Finn was about to smack Tony right on the jaw when Mr Morgan threw himself between them.

'Break it up, you two! And get off my premises with that sign!' he ordered. 'Any more of this nonsense and you're barred.'

His last words were addressed to Finn. Tony smirked at him.

'And you'll be looking for another job,' Mr Morgan warned Tony. Finn smirked back.

Finn's sign was looking rather the worse for wear, as were both Tony and Finn, who shrugged Tony's hand off his shoulder as if it was a tarantula.

'Don't worry, you haven't seen the last of me. I'll be back every day until I get my five hundred quid back. Now get out of my way,' Finn said, every muscle in his body tensed. He pushed Tony hard. 'Thanks to you, my business is probably in tatters and my relationship with Vicky is over.'

Tony made sure that Finn was well out of earshot before he said made his next remark.

'A good day's work then, all things considered,' he chortled, rubbing his hands together gleefully.

Lewis was waiting for Finn in the yard. 'Have you seen this?' he demanded. He was holding out the latest copy of the *Gazette*. Finn read it and ground his teeth at the same time.

'The rat!' he muttered. 'I might have guessed he'd already spoken to Tony to get his side of the story before he paid me a visit.'

'"I am just a prawn in his game", it says here,' Lewis said, pointing to Tony's words.

Finn had always suspected Lewis had dyslexic tendencies – particularly where pounds and pence were concerned. He frowned. 'Pawn, Lewis. It says pawn. I'll kill him, I swear to God.'

'It was a joke, Finn,' Lewis said. He'd never seen Finn so angry before.

'Well, it won't be a joke when I knock Tony Hutchinson's teeth out,' Finn snarled. 'And when I get Vicky back he'll be laughing on the other side of his face.'

CHAPTER FORTY-TWO

MAKING UP

Finn was missing Vicky. He decided to go round and tell her exactly how much. But what if she didn't even open the door to him? They'd both said some pretty harsh things. Well, if she wanted he would beg her to take him back. He'd never understood why so many people allowed their pride get in the way. Life was too short to let stupid things stand in the way of happiness. And let's face it, Tony was a stupid thing.

Far from being reluctant to talk to him, Vicky seemed overjoyed. She answered the door barefoot and seemed tiny to Finn, who was used to seeing her in her sexy heels.

'I thought I'd lost you for good,' she confessed, taking his hand and leading him to the kitchen. There was a bottle of white wine in one of those plastic coolers on the table, and just one glass.

'Drinking alone. Bad sign,' she said, reaching for another glass. 'We could take this through to the lounge.'

'Sounds like an excellent idea,' Finn said. As he leaned over her shoulder for the wine cooler, the familiar scent of her perfume lingered.

'Let's not fall out over Tony again, shall we, Finn? He told me you'd agreed to accept half the money he owed you for the catering so I hope that means you're both talking again.'

'Just,' Finn said. 'The odd monosyllable here and there, you know. Interspersed with a grunt now and again.'

Actually, his relationship with Tony continued to be as strained as one of his fruit purées.

'And has he told you his latest hare-brained scheme? About letting out rooms to that film crew that's in town? It means chucking his students out of their rooms. You can imagine how furious they are about it.'

Only ten minutes into the conversation and Tony was already the main topic. Finn really didn't want to think about him. Would it always be like this? he wondered. He let his eyes roam the length of Vicky's body where she lay, feet up, on the couch. He had an irresistible urge to massage her feet, which were tiny and beautifully pedicured, her toes painted pearly pink today.

He went over to be next to her and obligingly she moved up for him. Vicky sighed ecstatically as Finn began to rub the soles of her feet.

'Just what I need after an afternoon round the shops,' she said, closing her eyes. 'Bliss.'

'Good,' Finn said. 'So, Tony's plan. Does it have anything to do with that pile of rubbish in the garden? The caravan, I mean?'

Vicky laughed. 'That pile of rubbish in the garden, dear boy, has stood long service in this family. We used to go caravanning for family holidays when Tony was a boy in that. In the days before Tony's dad made his fortune and decided to swap both me and it for newer models.'

There was no bitterness in her voice. Finn lifted one foot and gently kissed her toes, one by one. 'Not a very good judge of vintage, your old man, if you ask me,' he said.

'Oh, Finn. You say such lovely things,' Vicky said. 'And you can be so thoughtful. I can't imagine my ex doing this. One day you'll make someone a very good husband.'

Finn suddenly stiffened, his eyes like saucers. Had he heard Vicky right, he wondered. Marriage? Surely she wasn't expecting him to propose marriage? Finn didn't do marriage. Marriage meant commitment. And look where that got people. He had a sudden urge to get up and leave – to scarper, in fact. But Vicky was asking him to help her get the caravan to Tony's before it got dark, so he could get it ready for his students. Until he'd done that, there was no way out.

CHAPTER FORTY-THREE

DECISIONS, DECISIONS

'So, how's it going between you and Victoria now you're back together?' Lewis asked Finn one morning. 'I must admit I've seen both of you looking happier.'

Finn stared straight ahead morosely.

'I think she wants me to ask her to marry me, mate,' he said at last, after a long silence.

Lewis was gobsmacked. 'And what about you? What do you want?'

Finn continued staring ahead at some distant point on the horizon. Lewis had never known Finn so uncommunicative. Prying information out of him today was like getting blood out of a stone. He decided to prompt him a bit.

'She's a lovely woman,' he said.

Finn nodded. And stared.

'You could do worse.'

Finn nodded again. Stared again.

'She's independent, strong, knows what she wants.'

Finally, Lewis's words provoked some reaction. 'Trouble is, mate, I think she wants me.'

Lewis was puzzled. 'And you're saying you don't want her, right?'

Finn did a bit more staring. 'Thing is, see, I don't know what I want.'

Lewis was beginning to understand Finn's dilemma. He decided to give Finn the benefit of his own experience. 'Take it from me, Finn,' he said, 'there's really nothing to be afraid of in commitment. Ruth and I are fully committed now and neither of us has ever felt happier.'

Finn shifted his gaze away from the spot he'd been staring at for the last quarter of an hour and finally looked Lewis full in the face.

'You reckon?' he said.

Lewis nodded enthusiastically.

'You really, really reckon?'

'Absolutely.'

Finn went back to staring his thousand-yard stare. 'I think I've just made a decision,' he said, after another silence in which Lewis was beginning to wonder if Finn would notice he wasn't there if he got up and walked off.

'Well?' He was glad he'd decided to stay and wait for it, whatever Finn's decision turned out to be. It was far too important to miss and he, Lewis Cunningham, would be the first to know.

'I've decided…'

'Yes?'

'I've decided…'

'Go on!'

'I've decided I'm going away for a few days,' Finn finally said. 'To think about it.'

'Right,' Lewis said, disappointed. 'You going straight away?'

He wasn't sure he could afford the time to hang around and wait for Finn's answer if it meant another one of those ponderous silences, but Finn suddenly snapped out of it.

'I'll be off to do some packing then. See you in a couple of days,' he said.

It was while he was packing a few things that he heard a commotion outside. Finn stuck his head out as an irate Tony loomed into view.

'What have I done now?' he asked. He didn't want to get involved in another row with Tony. He had more important things to think about.

'So my mum's not good enough for you, is she?' Tony yelled. 'Turned her down, did you?'

Finn had no idea what Tony was talking about and said so.

'I knew you'd break her heart one day. It was only a matter of time,' he continued. 'Well, let me tell you, she's worth ten of you and if you won't marry her then you're a bigger fool than I thought you were.'

Finn blinked. He'd missed a bit of the plot here. He wasn't quite sure what it was he should know but didn't – and Tony was starting to get on his nerves, standing there puffing and blowing like a man twice his age.

'You have seriously lost it, mate,' he said scornfully. 'I'm not surprised Vicky left your old man if he's anything like you. Which she says he is.'

Finn wasn't ready for the fearsome right hook that Tony planted on his jaw out of nowhere. For a second he reeled and almost lost his balance, but not before he managed to belt him back. Once again, Finn and Tony were at each other's throats and once again they were being pulled apart. Only this time it was Vicky who was doing her best to restore order, and not Mr Morgan.

'Finn! Tony! For God's sake, stop it! What's got into the pair of you? I demand an explanation immediately. I won't have you brawling over me like this!' she shrieked.

Finn put his hand up to the place where Tony had

hit him. 'You'd better ask your son what's going on,' he said. 'I haven't got a clue. I was about to do a bit of packing and––'

Vicky interrupted him, a hurt expression on her face. 'Packing?' she said.

'Running off, isn't he?' Tony said. 'The usual action of a man who can't make his mind up what he wants. Why you should propose marriage to a man like that is beyond me.'

Finn and Vicky exchanged puzzled looks. 'Whatever gave you the idea that I'd proposed marriage?' Vicky asked Tony.

'You did,' Tony said. 'When I came round last night to borrow that sleeping bag.'

Vicky's face suddenly cleared. 'Tony, you blockhead,' she sighed. 'That's not what I said at all. I said that Finn had left the house under some sort of impression that I was angling for him to ask me to marry him.'

'And you weren't?'

Finn and Tony barked the question simultaneously, both very much relieved when Vicky exclaimed: 'Of course not!'